<u>CROWN JEWEL</u>

THE BATTLE

FOR

THE FALKLANDS

By Peter von Bleichert

Books by Peter von Bleichert

Fiction

Dragon Fire: The Battle for the Falklands

Fourth Crisis: The Battle for Taiwan

Non-Fiction

Bleichert's Wire Ropeways

Blitz! Storming the Maginot Line

DEDICATION

Michael Muxie, III (in memoriam).

And, to those lost on both sides of the real Falklands War: 'Sleep well you Bonnie Lads/*Duerme bien valientes muchachos*.'

TABLE OF CONTENTS

CHARACTERS

ARGENTINE REPUBLIC:

Doctor Waldemar Amsel

Mayor (Major) Ezequiel Vargas

...and, Presidente de la Nación (President) Valeria Alonso; Almirante (Admiral) Javier Correa; Ministro de Defensa (Minister of Defense) Juan Cruz Gomez; & Capitán (Captain) Lucas Moreno.

UNITED KINGDOM:

Lieutenant Donnan Bruce

Major Scott Fagan

Aethelinda Jones

Anne Jones

Governor Roger Moody

His Royal Highness Prince Albert Richard George James Talbot of York

...and, the lads of 22 SAS Regiment, Squadron D, Air Troop; His Majesty King Edward IX; Eight-ball; Grey Bear; Henry Jones; Admiral Sir Reginald Nemeth; & the 'Warrahs' (Calvert, Fairbairn, Gubbins, McGregor, and Sykes).

UNITED STATES OF AMERICA

Commander Max Wolff

…and, SEAL Team 5.

NOTES

A British Overseas Territory, the Falkland Islands are a stark, wind-ripped South Atlantic archipelago some 400 miles east of Argentina's Patagonian coast, and 850 miles north of the Antarctic Circle. Comprising East Falkland, West Falkland, and 778 smaller islands, the Falkland Islands are roughly the size of the American State of Connecticut—about half the size of the country of Wales— and the capital is in the port city of Stanley on East Falkland. Falklanders are primarily of British, Chilean, and St. Helenian descent.

BRIEFING

The Argentine Republic claims sovereignty over the Falkland Islands.

Called *Las Islas Malvinas* by Argentinians, the archipelago is viewed as part of the South Atlantic Department of the Province of Tierra del Fuego.

The United Kingdom has never recognized this claim.

Although Falklanders have expressed a clear preference to remain under British rule, in hopes of easing tensions, during the 1960s, London engaged in talks with Argentine foreign missions. The talks, however, failed to reach any meaningful conclusion.

In the early 1980s, a ruthless dictatorship ruled Argentina. Accordingly, it suffered a crippling economic crisis. In an attempt to distract and unify its restive populace, Argentina initiated *Operación Rosario* on April 2, 1982, and invaded the Falklands.

Argentine forces outnumbered the British garrison 10-to-one. Resistance was rapidly subdued, and within hours, Argentine forces occupied Government House in Stanley—the Falklands' capital—and flew their flag over this symbol of British hegemony.

British Prime Minister Thatcher—dubbed the 'Iron Lady' by the Soviets—immediately denounced the invasion. She roused her military, organized and commenced Operation Corporate, and dispatched a Task Group to retake the islands.

After fierce air and naval battles, British forces landed on East Falkland. By mid-June of 1982, British marines and soldiers held the high ground around the capital city. Soon thereafter, the routed Argentine occupation forces surrendered.

Despite this clear-cut defeat, Argentina has continued to claim the South Atlantic archipelago as her own. In 1994, the Transitional Provisions of the Constitution of the Argentinian Nation were amended, thereby alleging 'legitimate and everlasting sovereignty' over *Las Islas Malvinas*, South Georgia, and the Sandwich Islands, as well as the corresponding maritime and insular areas.

With this legislation, the capture of said territories became a permanent and unswayable objective of the Argentine people…

The near-future…

PROLOGUE: CABAL

"*Wars are caused by undefended wealth.*"—Ernest Hemingway

Buenos Aires—Argentina's capital—grew up on the western shore of the estuary of the Río de la Plata. Sexy and alive, it bustled with nightlife. Its cityscape glowed restlessly in the dark, moonless night. People strolled in waterfront parks and among the eclectic mix of buildings.

They ambled along the city's wide avenues where traffic honked like impatient flocks of migrating geese, and scooters weaved in and out, buzzing like angry insects. Expansive plazas—cobblestone fields filled with fountains, statutes, trees, and vendors—allowed an escape from the jostling clamor. One of these urban oases was called *Plaza de Mayo*.

Named for the month of revolution, *Plaza de Mayo* honored the war that had brought independence from Spain. Ironically, this war of freedom had also brought shackles to Argentina's people as it concluded with the installation of the nation's first military government: *La Junta*.

On the plaza's eastern edge sat a baby pink palatial mansion, home to the President of Argentina. *La Casa Rosada*, as the home had been named, featured a North Hall where tall, arched windows let the light of day flood in, but could stop all else, including bullets. The President of Argentina walked within this hall. Her name: Valeria Alonso. As president and commander-in-chief of the nation's armed forces, she presided over the gathered nation's Military Council. Her high-heels clicked on the stone floor as she stalked along the long, rectangular table, lecturing those assembled in the stuffy, bright room.

Those assembled there included Minister of Defense Juan Cruz Gomez, and Admiral Javier Correa, among others. President Alonso tossed her hair back as she spoke, intimidatingly locking eyes with each of her subordinates. Her piercing eyes were dark brown, just like her long hair; both features gifts from her mother. However, those eyes also flashed with her father's keen intellect.

Her father, Doctor Waldemar Amsel, sat in his office—a concrete bunker far below the streets of Buenos Aires—and watched his daughter on a video screen.

Dr. Amsel was once known as SS Obersturmführer Amsel of Occupied Poland's Sobibor extermination camp, a place where the crematorium ovens stayed busy and ash fell with the winter snow, tinting the ground a sickly grey. In the waning days of World War II, while the vengeful Russians were closing in on his death camp, he and the other officers had commandeered a supply truck, taking it skidding along Polish back roads with the 'Reds' on their heels all the while.

A droning engine then announced the arrival of marauding aircraft, and, as they raced through woods and along snow-covered fields, a Stormovik found them, dove hard, and strafed their vehicle. The bullets ripped through the canvas roof of the old Mercedes, and then into Amsel's legs. With Amsel bleeding heavily and barely conscious, his loyal cadre took him to a doctor in Genoa, and, after a week lying bandaged in bed, he and his cohorts received Red Cross passports.

Amsel was wheeled to the harbor and put aboard the transport ship *Dodero*. This rusting tramp was a cog in the intricate machinery of the 'Ratline,' the network that delivered fleeing Nazis to South America and other points around the globe. That rainy day at the Genovese docks, *Dodero* set sail for Buenos Aires.

Amsel then healed during the long, slow voyage. When they arrived on the South American coast, he was met by Argentina's Rodolfo Freude, an advisor to Juan Domingo Peron.

Despite many surgeries in Argentina's best hospitals, Amsel remained wheelchair-bound. It was in this chair that Amsel had turned inward, trained his substantial intellect, and nurtured knowledge with a voracious appetite for the written word.

Amsel sat among the rows of tall tome-filled shelves at the University of Buenos Aires's library, where spears of light pierced the reading room's arched windows and illuminated the piles of leather-bound books that surrounded him. Surrounded by paper ramparts, he greedily consumed the contents of classics and revolutionaries alike. All the while, the beams of day light crossed the desk and climbed the shelves, marking the passage of so much time.

It was within this library that Amsel was noticed by, and met, an Argentinian student named Beatriz.

Beatriz had looked beyond Amsel's shattered legs, past his cold eyes, and peered deep into Amsel's mind. It was there, among the twisted folds and spongy matter that Beatriz became enamored with him. It was there, in the darkness of a foreign mind, that Beatriz was seduced. One night—fascinated by the immobile professor who had taught her more about her world and self than any other—Beatriz had straddled and mounted Amsel. Their daughter, Valeria, was born nine months later.

One day, not long after, Beatriz found Amsel's SS Totenkopfverbände pin. The 'Death's Head' had adorned Amsel's black cap as he ordered women and children to the showers. It was the only memento of those 'happy days' he had kept. His vanity backfired, however, as Beatriz found and studied the silver skull and crossbones. With Valeria squirming and screaming in her bassinette, Beatriz confronted Amsel and, during the argument, Amsel stabbed Beatriz. Her frail young body then folded on the kitchen floor where she bled out.

After this 'cooking accident,' as the police had labeled it, Amsel raised Valeria on his own, providing her with an education, several languages, and the belief that power was life's ultimate goal. Valeria had grown quickly as Amsel's temples greyed, and as his sharp nose came to support thick glasses. Meanwhile, he had become a trusted advisor to the Argentine government.

Amsel was admired for his cold, hard political advice and vast repository of information. Soon thereafter, the government had the university bestow an honorary doctorate upon him, and it was from this point on that the former Nazi became Doctor Waldemar Amsel, or, to those who sought his counsel, simply, 'Herr Doctor.'

Like any good Nazi, Amsel despised Communism, and was happy to be instrumental in the design and implementation of Operation Condor, Argentina's *Guerra Sucia*—the 'Dirty War'—during which Amsel handpicked most of those to be 'disappeared.' When Argentina's economy faltered and indignation spread, threatening the dictatorship, Admiral Anaya convinced then-president General Galtieri that an invasion of *Las Islas Malvinas* was just the nationalist ticket they needed. Amsel, with first-hand insight into British determination, and with an understanding of their military capabilities at the time, warned the regime against such an undertaking. Although history had shown these men wrong and Amsel right, they had all come and gone. Amsel, however, remained. *As for the British*, Amsel thought, *that was then, and this is now*. Amsel re-tuned his gaze to the video screen. Valeria flowed around the room and the squirming ministers.

Valeria had taken her mother's surname for political purposes. Thanks to her father's powerful allies, she experienced a meteoric rise in the National Congress and soon rose to the presidency. Through his daughter, Amsel—a master marionetteer—had pulled the strings of the Argentine Republic. He watched as Valeria addressed the Military Council. Despite his advanced age, he yielded to his one admitted weakness and lit a cigarette. Amsel smiled broadly. He was filled with pride in his daughter; his creation; his progeny. Close to making those who had toppled the Reich bleed, Amsel overflowed with happiness, and he chuckled. Through wisps of blue tobacco smoke, Amsel focused on the office video screen and turned up the volume on the small desktop speaker. Although his Spanish was permeated by a Germanic accent and never quite became fluent, and despite Valeria's native rattling diction, Amsel understood and savored each of her words.

"Since the War of the South Atlantic…" Valeria's husky voice demanded attention, and invited no questions. "…the British armed forces have been gutted, and their precious Royal Navy is a former shadow of itself." She had studied the speeches of Bill Clinton, Adolf Hitler, Benito Mussolini, Barack Obama, Evita Peron, and Ronald Reagan—all speakers she and her father admired—and borrowed articulation and nuances from each, incorporating them into her own style. While the words were carefully compiled by her father, Valeria's presentation was totally her own, and was made all the more effective by her stunning beauty.

"The aircraft carriers *Hermes* and *Invincible*—two names we will forever despise—have been scrapped," she said. "Their successors—the white elephants of the new *Queen Elizabeth*-class—have been delayed and plagued by technical problems, and the rest of the British fleet represents half the numbers of the 1980s." Valeria paused

to stare at Admiral Correa. He fidgeted as these points to

sank in. To the admiral's relief, Valeria moved her laser

gaze to the air force's brigadier general, and continued:

"The Harrier jump-jets have been retired, and the new F-35s

meant to replace them are broken albatrosses, lacking in

numbers and are perpetually grounded with one difficulty

after another. The British air force no longer has any long-

range strike capability, and their army and marines are

exhausted from combat in Iraq and Afghanistan. On top of

this, their economy is in recession, and the British people

are tired from years of expeditionary combat in

questionable wars; wars that have drained both treasure and

blood." Valeria cracked a smile. Although happy to let

blame fall on the usual suspects, she knew Argentina's

Secretaría de Inteligencia—the nation's intelligence

service—had been responsible for at least half a dozen

'terrorist' attacks against British forces in foreign theaters. Like setting plaster, her face again hardened. Valeria continued, "Our own economy is…unstable. This is not due to any fault of our own. It is, however, due to an international banking system dominated by London and New York. A system that punishes us like naughty children. A system that threatens to undermine the hard work and deserved glory of our people." The volume of Valeria's voice had risen to emphasize this last word, and then quieted again. "And what is the solution?" She did not wait for volunteered guesses, but provided her own short answer: "Oil and the revenues it brings."

Six months later…

1: KALAT

"Innocence does not find near so much protection as guilt."—Francois de La Rochefoucauld

The Apache, like most United States combat helicopters, had been named for native peoples of the North American continent. The tribe had deservedly been known as fierce warriors, cunning tacticians, and for being led by strategic-thinking chiefs. The Apache assault helicopter was a black and foreboding dragonfly; a formidable tank-killer and general ground support aircraft. The choppers sported air-to-surface missiles, and, slung beneath its sleek fuselage, an automatic cannon. One of these awesome machines sat on the asphalt and concrete tarmac of Camp Bastion, Helmand Province, Afghanistan.

It had been built by AgustaWestland in the United Kingdom, and belonged to 662 Squadron, Royal Army Air Corps. The helicopter featured a radar dome atop its four-bladed main rotor. Slabs of thick ballistic cockpit glass surrounded two figures moving within. In the rear pilot's seat fidgeted His Royal Highness Prince Albert Richard George James Talbot of York—Prince Albert to most.

With sharp features, beady piercing eyes, a tall taut frame, and reddish blonde hair, Prince Albert was well-known for his cheeky grin, youthful cannabis indulgence and pub-crawling, and his healthy disdain for the formalities of royal title. Despite endless Al-Qaeda and Taliban threats against his life, Albert thrived in the warzone.

Although he had once harbored dreams of becoming a painter or writer, his royal station, as well as a rigid father who respected no such silly pursuits, pushed him to armed service. After successfully completing general infantry and flight training, he had no intention of sitting by as his mates deployed to Afghanistan and Iraq. As Coróna Principem—Crown Prince—there were no allowances for Albert to be in such danger. Only after many heated arguments and emotion-laden threats to abdicate his title, had his father, the King, relented. With Afghanistan deemed safer than insurgent-ridden Iraq, Albert had been permitted to deploy on condition that he have his own security detail, that he assume a nom du guerre, and, should intelligence indicate the enemy had become aware of his presence, that he return home immediately. Therefore, Prince Albert—Captain Albert Talbot—became Captain Albert Smith, and deployed to Afghanistan where he was paired with his beloved Apache, as well as his vetted cockpit mate, co-pilot/gunner Lieutenant Donnan Bruce.

With bright blue eyes, a round face, ruddy skin, and a balding head that, in patches, was covered by black razor-hewn stubble, Donnan stood as a stocky Scotsman from Inverness, and a hardened veteran of the Gulf War. He was also one of the few to know 'Captain Smith's' true identity. Segregated on base with Albert, Donnan had come to enjoy the private meals, cushy barracks, and ample supplies that came with living with a Prince. He often joked he should get a title, suggesting it as 'Donnan, Count of Helmand' with a coat of arms made up of two darts crossed before a bottle of beer. When at work, however, Donnan became deadly serious, a ruthless gunner who never hesitated to kill. In the Apache's tandem cockpit, these two men played their control panels, and went through the pre-flight checklist.

Albert looked outside for a moment. The sun had set the sky ablaze in reds and oranges. In the purple-tinted blue on-high, white streaks marked where American B-52s had made their way on some nameless bombing run against mountain redoubts. He sighed and made inputs to the three digital displays arrayed before him. He also checked the flight systems and programmed the navigation computer with destination coordinates and flight-path waypoints. He lowered and adjusted a helmet-mounted monocular lens— what American Apache pilots affectionately called the 'Colonel Klink'—and centered it before his right eye. With an electronic flicker, imagery filled the monocle and flooded Albert's view.

The Apache's nose turret sported an unblinking mechanical eye that fed the monocle with an inhuman view of the world: Even in the last of the hot day's sunlight, body heat and vehicle engines appeared as bright white against a dark-grey background. Albert turned his head and cockpit sensors detected the movement of his helmet, tracking the nose turret in unison. He watched as a ground technician strolled up and signaled readiness. He was to guide the Apache into the sky. Beginning to sweat, Albert started the cockpit fans. Although the blown air was filtered, aviation gas fumes and the dry stink of Afghanistan's air—what they all called the 'Big Latrine' for its sun-stewed aroma—was sucked inside.

"Is that roses I smell, mate?" the helmet speaker crackled with Donnan's thick accent.

"Smells like Highlander to me," Albert rebutted.

As usual, Donnan's laugh was deep and hearty. The quips sent at each other had a calming effect, and counteracted the shakes-inducing adrenalin. Albert often jabbed at his cockpit companion just to hear that laugh; a laugh that sounded like it belonged to a ten-foot giant. Donnan snorted and reported: "All ready." They got a thumbs-up from the man outside, too. Albert did a final scan.

Electronics, hydraulics, and other parameters for the Apache's two big Rolls-Royce Turbomeca turbo-shaft engines were all in the green. Albert took the aircraft's collective and cyclic controls in his gloved hands and engaged the main and tail rotors. The helicopter, anxious to take flight, vibrated excitedly. Shimmering heat blew out of the exhausts mounted either side of the fuselage, and the rotors began to rotate, rhythmically chopping at the air. The ground technician twirled an arm. The gesture signified good spin-up. The technician then indicated the Apache was clear of any ground obstructions and had authorization for departure. Albert lifted the collective.

The neutral rotor blades articulated and bit into the air, pushing air down and creating lift, the phenomena Albert called the 'power of up.' The Apache leapt off the tarmac, rose to 50 feet, hovered, turned, and dipped its nose toward the craggy hills that lined the northeastern horizon. The man on the ground saluted, and Albert contacted the tower.

Albert was assigned a departure lane that would get his aircraft safely through other inbound and outbound American, Australian, and British air traffic. Once outside the wire, the brightly-lit base perimeter fell behind. Donnan and Albert found themselves swallowed by the stone-age darkness of Afghanistan.

Scanning ahead with night vision, Albert spotted the heat forms of a camel caravan, fires from a small village, and a man on a hill. This man, dismissed as just another peasant in the mountains, reported the helicopter's departure and general heading to his Taliban buddies. Albert flew the Apache along the line demarked by the navigation computer. They were on their way to support an assault on the centuries-old Jugroom Fort.

Albert checked the mission computer. He noted that his flight was on-course and on-time. Their Apache was tasked to rendezvous with an American armed scout helicopter—a Kiowa—and be under the control of one of their Forward Air Controllers already dug in on the heights above the ancient fortress.

Dry mud bricks comprised Jugroom's outer wall. Upon a central earthen motte, there stood a collection of fortified buildings that the Taliban and foreign fighters— mostly Arabs and Chechens—used to store weapons caches, to feed and house fighters, and to protect the season's opium crop until it could be moved out by donkey. Tonight's assault was dual purpose: confiscate or destroy the drugs, and capture or kill as many insurgents as possible. Also, intelligence had indicated the presence of an Al-Qaeda leader. This leader was not high on the totem pole, though worthy of interrogation if caught. The American colonel who delivered the mission briefing had remarked, "No one would cry if this Al-Qaeda fucker happened to be killed;" adding, "Guantanamo's all full up."

Albert flew his Apache nap-of-the earth, a very low-altitude mode of flight utilized to avoid enemy detection in a high-threat environment. He consulted a tactical diagram strapped to his knee, and noted symbols that represented the small village that sat in the shadow of the old fort.

A mere collection of hovels and shacks, the village relied on the fort's spring for drinking and irrigation water, and splayed just beyond a rampart built around Jugroom's brick perimeter wall. The village was danger-close and civilians were at home. As always, and since the village could not be warned beforehand, briefings included a caution against collateral damage. While Albert knew this was for purposes of 'hearts and minds,' his avoidance of the village would be for the women and children; the same women and children the Taliban had a tendency to shelter behind when threatened.

"Five miles," Albert called out.

"Right," Donnan grunted. That one simple word indicated Donnan was ready with the helicopter's 30 millimeter Chain Gun, its Hellfire missiles, and its 70 millimeter CRV7 folding-fin rockets. A green indicator light on a cockpit panel told Donnan that, in the dome above the main rotor, the Apache's Longbow acquisition and targeting radar was warmed up and ready for business.

The Apache hovered behind a rocky hillock, its gear tires barely three feet from the ground.

"Okay, let's see what we can see." Albert brought the Apache above the precipice, allowing their night vision sensors and optical systems to do a quick scan of the terrain.

Jugroom Fort was visible, and atop its ramparts, they could see Taliban fighters guarding the approaches. On the cockpit screens, heat from lots of US Marines was also visible. They had formed up out of view of the fort, and this mass was ready to begin the assault. Dropping the aircraft down again, Albert checked his watch and announced the attack would commence in three minutes.

"Roger," said Donnan. They would open the proceedings with a Hellfire missile, the weapon blasting a breach in the old mud wall and making a nice hole for the marines to pour through, before fanning out within the enemy compound. Just before the Hellfire arrived, Donnan would guide his cannon fire along the rampart's crenellations, hosing the enemy with 30 millimeter bullets.

"Okay, mate, no stray rounds in that village," Albert reminded Donnan.

"Roger," Donnan acknowledged. "I'll use the laser designator for Hellfire," Donnan announced. This meant Albert would have to keep the Apache's nose above cover for the duration of the missile's flight. Although the Longbow radar could guide the Hellfire, the laser—when the air was clear of dust like tonight—directed the missile to within inches of the desired point of impact, making it far more accurate.

"One minute," Albert counted.

Flashing panel lights indicated the Chain Gun had awakened, and that a Hellfire was ready for launch.

"Ten seconds…five, four, three, two, one."

The Apache unmasked. The cockpit screens showed the heat of the sallying Americans. Donnan energized the Apache's laser designator. The Hellfire's single menacing eye spotted the laser's invisible beam dancing on the fort's rampart. With a whoosh and a bang, the Hellfire ignited and slid from its wing rail, speeding off to its target. Albert kept the Apache steady to maintain beam integrity. With the missile away, Donnan wasted no time opening up with his Chain Gun. The Apache shook, and the cannon rounds impacted along the top of the fort's wall.

One-by-one, enemy fighters fell from their firing positions. In his night vision screen, Albert saw one Talib stand to fire at the Marines. Hit by the Chain Gun's large bullets, a light green mist appeared where the fighter had once been. Then the Hellfire slammed into the wall and exploded.

Dry mud blasted airborne. When the smoke cleared, the fort's perimeter had yawned open. American mortar crews landed rounds in the compound, and the infantry charged in behind the impacts. The radio crackled. The voice of the Yank in charge of the assault ordered the

Apache to hold fire as his men came within range of the fort and the helicopter's deadly armaments.

The missile launch and cannon fire lit up his Apache like a Hollywood premiere. Albert used the respite to bound to a new position. He banked and broke hard, finding and settling in behind an outcropping. Although anti-aircraft missiles were scarce in these parts, everybody and his mother seemed to own the dreaded nemesis of the helicopter: rocket-propelled grenades.

"Bulldog 31, in cover position," Albert transmitted. This told the marines that he had moved, and was ready to provide suppressive fire by request. The American commander responded a moment later, shouting over the racket of small arms fire. Albert got the Apache back up, and brought its nose sensors from behind the rocks.

The Americans streamed into the fort. Albert could see the white splotches of their body heat. Viewed in the night vision screen, each blob of white light was a man, and each was far from home, and each missed a woman and children who they had left behind to wonder and to worry. A suited politician, sitting comfortably behind a big wooden desk, had sent each of these white shapes on the green screen. Albert felt for these simple men. They loved country and guns, and had flown into Afghanistan to do right by both. The screen went white. Marines had chucked a grenade through a window opening and set off a weapons cache. As the blinding flash cleared, Albert watched a flickering black shape move into the scene.

A medevac Black Hawk helicopter landed in an adjacent field. The white blobs carried several comrades to the machine. The men on stretchers had been hit by a heavy machine gun positioned upon one of the fort's parapets. The enemy gun had been fired for a just a moment. The gun's brief moment of glory was quickly silenced by return fire, but it inflicted damage nonetheless. On a dark side of the fort, Donnan and Albert watched a group of enemy fighters scurry from the protection of the fort. The shapes moved along a drainage ditch that led to the adjacent village.

"Caution: enemy on the move; southern quadrant. I see several figures headed toward the village," Albert transmitted on the open band. The cockpit intercom clicked.

"Should I take them out?" Donnan asked Albert's permission to engage the new targets.

"Negative, too close to the village. Let the marines get them." Donnan trained the Chain Gun in their direction, anyway. Using his gunner's night vision system to keep the targeting reticle centered on the lead figure, Donnan could see the unique outlines of hot Kalashnikovs. Also, at least one fighter had something across his shoulder. The weapon's silhouette suggested that of a Russian-built rocket-propelled grenade.

"Bulldog 31," the American commander called out. "Put fire on that group."

"Negative, too close to village," Albert responded almost instantaneously.

"That's an order, Bulldog 31." The American was in command and knew it. Interpreting his screen, Donnan told Albert that the enemy was getting in a vehicle parked outside a village shack.

"Sir, our Al-Qaeda target is likely among this bunch," Donnan posited. "Request Hellfire."

Albert took a moment, and then authorized Donnan to use the air-to-ground missile. Donnan locked the Longbow radar on the vehicle.

"Longbow lock-up. Firing." Another Hellfire screamed away. The missile skipped down the hillside at the vehicle. Both men watched their night vision screens. The target pulled forward several feet. It stopped in front of a small brick building, and several figures emerged and moved to the SUV's open rear doors.

The heat signatures of this second group were smaller, and one seemed to clutch a small bear-shaped object. Donnan knew the UN was fond of handing out teddy-bears to the children of Afghanistan.

"Bloody hell," Donnan exclaimed, "I think there are women…and a child." Knowing full well that the seeker in the Hellfire's nose would continue to guide it in anyway, Albert ordered Donnan to shut down the radar.

In what seemed an eternity, both men watched as the family scrambled into the target vehicle. The SUV began to roll again. It moved several feet before the Hellfire knocked on its front passenger-side door. Albert and Donnan watched in horror. The cockpit screens flashed white, blinded by the Hellfire's high-explosive anti-tank warhead.

"Good shooting, Bulldog," came over the radio.

Slumped in their cockpit harnesses, both men sat in stunned silence. These two warriors had just become murderers.

The Apache drifted slightly. The tips of its rotor came dangerously close to a rock wall. Albert snapped out of it and corrected the helicopter's attitude.

A summer shower had cooled London, making the city glisten in the sunshine. Grey clouds cleared, and beams of light shone on the dome of Saint Paul's cathedral, the spires of Westminster Abbey, the skyscrapers of Canary Wharf, and the iron span of Tower Bridge. The Thames River snaked beneath the myriad of bridges that spanned it, and the bright day made its mud-brown waters sparkle.

Below the streets of the metropolis stretched the cylindrical tunnels of the 'Tube,' London's underground railroad.

At the Tube's Embankment Station, a government official got off a silver train, and, minding the gap, stepped onto the platform. As she moved toward the station's exit, the official came upon someone reading a newspaper. Next to the pudgy fingers that clasped the front page, she saw a picture of the Prince in full military dress and a headline that declared: PRINCE ALBERT IN AFGHANISTAN. She gasped and hurried to her Whitehall office.

Within the soot-covered Ministry of Defence building, she burst into the minister's office.

"Have you seen today's paper?" she asked the minister.

"Yes, yes. Damnit, yes," he grumbled back.

"Al-Qaeda and the Taliban will get word."

"I know, I know. It's time to bring Prince Albert home. Make it so," the minister ordered.

"Yes, sir," the official sighed. She would have a long day of phone calls ahead, though she would have Prince Albert safely home within a week. She got to work.

The minster leaned over his desk. He would request a cup of tea later, but in the meantime, he thumbed through the day's dispatches.

On top of the pile of papers, the first report stated that a UK-based petroleum company had made a significant discovery of light oil in the resource-rich seabed that surrounded the Falkland Islands.

"You do not look well," King Edward said to his oldest son. Even though Albert sat, arrayed in full military dress and seated within the splendor of Buckingham Palace's blue drawing room, he knew the comment was likely true. Since the incident at Jugroom, Albert had been drinking heavily. He and Donnan started indulging just after the battle, just as soon as they landed at Camp Bastion. Their first victim was a bottle of single malt whiskey Donnan had kept in his foot locker. After the golden elixir was gone, it was downhill like a wheel of cheese for them both, as they dispensed with Russian vodka, Indian gin, and even a cube of black hash.

Donnan had punched the Special Air Service bloke who tried to slow them down, and got a broken arm for his mistake. When flight orders came in, Albert claimed to be sick, and an American doctor who had come to examine him took one whiff of the fumes that emanated from his pores, he shook his head, and signed the medical release. By then, all of Camp Bastion—as well as all of Afghanistan for that matter—knew about the Prince's presence. With the news, half the Brits on base had tried to leave gifts of delicacies and liquors at Albert's private barracks, though the SAS contingent never let anyone get too close to what the whole camp had previously believed to be just an air conditioned supply shed.

"Thank you, Your Majesty," Albert finally acknowledged the King's statement.

At the moment, Albert hated his father only slightly more than he hated himself. Despite the red and gold carpet, and the portraits of ancestors whose heavy judgmental gaze fell upon him, Albert wanted to spit on the floor. He swallowed hard, instead. He closed his eyes to fight off a headache that felt like a creature moving within the folds of his brain. In the pink darkness behind his lids, Albert saw the missile hit the Talibani SUV. He had seen this image—dreamt about it—every night. In the vision, the little girl emerged from the fire, bloodied and charred, and asked Albert what she had done to make him so mad.

Among the room's fine art was a globe made in 1750. Albert remembered playing with it as a child, spinning it, and when it stopped turning, he would look to see what exotic locale had ended up under his thumb. Regardless of the place, he would always say to his older brother: "Perhaps we will go there someday." Upon it, he saw the Durrani Empire—present-day Afghanistan. In the late eighteenth century, its borders had stretched into Iran, as well as modern-day India and Pakistan.

"When we are in private, you may address me as, 'Father,'" the King said.

"Yes, Your Majesty." Albert's reply was distant and monotone.

King Edward huffed with frustration. His first born son, Henry, had been killed during a stag hunt at the Royal Hunting Reserve at Balmoral Castle. It had been the King who found his son's body with a hole in his chest, slumped over a rock by the River Dee. At his son's feet was the dropped and discharged rifle, a lick of blue smoke wafting from its bore.

Albert had always been the King's afterthought, second place to Henry's accomplishments and talents. Now he was heir to all the empire and kingdom. Although he always loved Albert, the King felt let down by his younger boy. After all, a King's progeny should not exhibit the frailties of other common folk; he must be hard, strong, and adhere to a timeless preordained model. When Albert's musings of art and literature had replaced business, hunting, and warfare as preferred loves, the King concluded that he and Albert were not cut from the same jib. A butting of heads and stubborn wills consumed their relationship ever since. The boy had decided his path, and the King found every flaw as an excuse to stab at the heart of the one he was meant to nurture. What the King would never know, never realize, is that he too had become just like his own father.

Once, King Edward had had his own spark of desire within; a desire to live his own life and walk his own path. This spark had been readily snuffed. The once young Prince Edward had longed for the embrace and acceptance of his own father. However, he had been pushed away, frozen cold by pretense and appearances, forever corrupted with a centuries-old attitude that had broken many a royal son.

Even when in the same room, Albert and his father might as well have been a million miles apart. Although his father knew nothing of the incident at Jugroom Fort, Albert's return home—simply a matter of security—was viewed by King Edward as a failure of sorts, a retreat; a defeat on the field of battle.

The King did not see the medals on his son's chest, the badge of the army air corps, nor his pilot's insignia, or the blood on his hands. He saw only that his son had been forced home. Albert's warm, dark, brown eyes—the eyes of his mother—looked deep into the blue eyes of his father, the Germanic eyes inherited from the royal bloodline of Europe. Looking into the cold pools, Albert realized his father would have preferred him to come home in a flag-draped coffin, preferred it to his running from a cadre of sheep-herding rifle-toting peasants. At that moment, Albert also realized that his father would have preferred it, had he been the one to die that day by the River Dee.

Albert was about to say it was not his choice to return from Afghanistan. However, like many explanations before, Albert knew his words would be futile, would float in the still air of the palace's grandeur, and echo softly among the frescos and ornate ceilings before fading to silence. He adjusted his tight collar.

The scratchy confines of Albert's uniform became a symbol of his bondage; bondage to a life for which he did not ask, a life he would trade for nearly any other. In that moment, Albert wished he could see his mother once more. He wanted to be a little boy again, held in her comforting arms, crying over the injustices that kept a free spirit bound, the hell of a life that sucked animus until one was a beaten shell of the child that once was, a zombie that shambled through day-to-day tortures with a forced smile painted on wrinkled skin. Albert felt the worst of the human condition: hopelessness. However, such feelings ran counter to all he had been taught as an Englishman—stiff upper-lip and all— Albert wanted to embrace this hopelessness. He wanted to run, to fly, to hide at the ends of the Earth. He wanted to trade places with that little girl. He wanted to be dead.

"Albert, you will go to Stanley in the Falklands," King Edward said to the floor. Really, the King did not care where it was he was sending his son, so long as it is from his sight.

"Yes, Your Majesty," Albert replied with a sigh.

2: DOGO

"No one becomes depraved all at once."—Juvenal

There was a building in the heart of downtown Buenos Aires, on a street not far from the main square in the Monserrat neighborhood of the central capital. Constructed in 1929, the neo-classic building included a collection of antennae that jutted from its mansard roof, but was, to all outward appearances, otherwise stuck in time. Twenty-odd stories in height, pedestrians tended to quicken their pace as they passed it by.

Known as the home of Argentina's National Directorate of Strategic Military Intelligence, the building hid a long, dark history that the bright lights flooding its façade could not wash away. Its upper floors held the aroma of wooden shelves and old books. Below street level, however, the thick air of its basement reeked of sweat, urine, and blood. It was here that shadows lived; shadows of the past that still crept along hallways and stopped to listen at doorways. Among these shadows was a stooped, wheel chair-bound form.

Doctor Amsel sat huddled in one of the building's antechambers, staring at a flickering black & white video screen. Since Valeria was not around to scold him, he was smoking again. As he took a long draw on the crackling American tobacco, he watched one of his best at work, listening to the proceedings through a wall-mounted speaker.

Major Ezequiel Vargas, of the elite 601 Commando Company, struck the prisoner. Caught near a military facility, the bloodied Chilean man was quickly labeled a spy and taken into custody. Albeit just an innocent tourist, the prisoner would never see his children, wife, or homeland again.

Argentina had never forgotten Chile's support of the British during the Falklands War, and Vargas would make sure to properly remind this man of the fact. In the middle of the dark damp interrogation room, beneath the lifeless stare of the ceiling-mounted camera, the Chilean slouched naked and bound to a cold metal chair, his face swollen and cracked from repeated punches. Vargas landed another, knocking the Chilean from semi-consciousness into blackness. The victim awakened several minutes later when Vargas poured ice water over his head.

"*Bueno, mi amigo,*" Vargas said. He raised one of his favorite motivational instruments: a power drill. He revved its electric motor, spun its bit, pointed it at the Chilean's hand, and slowly pushed it closer to flesh. Even though the prisoner could hear the tool and he saw it approaching, he was unable to utter a word. Instead, he gurgled. And then, he screamed.

The bellow passed through the thick stone walls as if they were made of paper. Amsel pushed a button on his control panel.

The interrogation room speaker crackled with Amsel's familiar German-accented Spanish. Vargas had been summoned.

Although proud to be favored—giving him purpose and justification for his methodology—Vargas still had to hide his annoyance at the disturbance. Splattered with blood, Vargas dutifully went to his superior and mentor.

"I have an important job for you," Amsel said.

Vargas nodded, saluted, and said: *"Entiendo, jefe."*

◊◊◊◊

Cerro General Belgrano loomed the tallest peak among the Sierra de Famatina Mountains of Argentina.

Snow-capped and jagged, this alp stood surrounded by smaller crags. The mount, named for an Argentine economist, lawyer, politician, and military leader who had taken part in the Argentine Wars of Independence and had created the new nation's flag, stood surrounded by young peaks, not yet rounded by time, rain, and wind. The smaller peaks surrounded the tallest, most majestic one, sitting about it in a circle, as though eager to hear a riveting story.

Vargas sat there too, on an outcropping that perched inconsequentially partway up that big rock, overlooking the valley town of Chilecito, a small city surrounded by rock and farm fields that seemed out of place among the dry heights.

Vargas looked up at Belgrano's heights with awe and inspiration. The wind at its peak grabbed and pulled the snow, forming a white plume that feathered into the atmosphere. At the snow line, where the stark rock became ice-covered, were the ore fields of *La Mejicana*. Vargas took a deep, refreshing breath that tasted of new snow. Light-headed from the altitude, Vargas felt good. He knelt to inspect a purple flower growing from among cracks in the rock.

He knelt beside it and watched the plant sway in the breeze. Vargas's bruised knuckles closed about the flower's delicate stem. If not for the clanking of the Cable Carril—an antique wire ropeway that climbed into the heights—he would be surrounded by dead silence.

Although the Cable Carril once transported rich ore from the towering heights down to the railroad located in the steep valley floor, the old system was now relegated to moving batches of tourists to a trailhead located at the ropeway's first station. Vargas watched a gondola approaching. As he waited for it to arrive, he thought about his wife.

Vargas had loved her even more than he loved

Argentina. The day she died in a fiery car crash, his unborn

child nestled in her creamy-white belly, Vargas had

changed, become different, a much darker man. No longer

was he a simple soldier. Instead, Vargas became a killer

driven by vicious anger at a seemingly uncaring God. Yes,

he had been raised as part of a devoutly Catholic family, but

when the coroner had pulled back the fluid-stained sheet

from his wife's corpse, exposing her crisp and blackened

face, Vargas felt an electric shock within and experienced a

black epiphany: There was no God, and the universe was a

cold, neutral, indifferent place. Vargas had killed

shamelessly ever since, daring the supposed deity to prove

His existence by taking and punishing a once-pious man.

As always, during peaceful moments, when surrounded by

the beauty of the land, Vargas longed for the man he once

was, to be good and forthright again. He shoved these

thoughts quickly shoved away, caught by the breeze, and

supplanted by a question: Was it a daughter or son that had

died in his wife's womb, starved of blood and oxygen,

squirming as its newly developing organs shut down?

Vargas wanted to simultaneously cry with sadness and

scream with anger. He was convinced that, if their child

had been a girl, she would have been as beautiful as his

wife. And, if a boy, he would be strong and focused like his

dad. Somewhere in his soul, Vargas knew it was a little girl

that had died with his wife that day, and this knowledge

made him all the angrier. What more, after all, is a father

meant to do but protect a sweet, innocent little girl? *There

can be no divine being*, he concluded. Vargas was

convinced of this. For no such supernatural spirit of good

could let such things happen. And, if there was no God, no

Heaven, or Hell, Vargas could do as his nature told him,

and as those with a better understanding of the world

ordered him to do. The sound of the old wire ropeway jarred Vargas from his troubled thoughts.

Among the Cable Carril's load of tourists was a man Vargas recognized, a face he had studied; memorized, a member of the Argentine National Congress. He was an outspoken member who openly criticized the administration of President Valeria Alonso. While most other Argentinians wished to forget, this man had pushed for more information, information on those that had disappeared in the time of *La Junta*. The wire ropeway slowed, and the station attendant glided the gondola and its load of tourists into the station. The riders disembarked.

They milled about in clumps and inspected the old engineering work. The tourists dispersed, spreading out over the outcropping and drifting toward the natural beauty beyond. They shot pictures with cameras and they gawked at the wondrous view. One oblivious woman had her face

63

buried in a smartphone. Her thumbs typed another meaningless message. An older couple spoke about the days when the town of Chilecito rode the crest of a mining boom. The old Cable Carril had hauled load after load of copper, gold, and silver from the mines of *La Mejicana*, and delivered them to steaming trains on the valley floor.

The crowd of tourists thinned. Some headed to the trail while others wandered toward a field of grass and wildflowers that danced in the breeze.

Vargas nodded hello to a young woman who had noticed his Latin good looks but then, seeing the scar just beneath his close cropped hair, she winced. Vargas's smile widened. The taught lips revealed one gold-capped tooth. Then Vargas flicked his tongue at her. Her flirtatious interest suddenly became uncomfortable recoil, and she turned and walked away. Vargas saw the congressman again, now alone and wandering about.

The congressman's domain was *La Rioja* Province. Despite rabblerousing, he was free of care or concern as he began his weekly constitutional: a brisk hike along the old road that snaked along the path of the ropeway. Like a stalking cat, Vargas trailed, not far behind.

The congressman stopped beneath an iron tower perched precariously next to a steep drop. It held the wire rope up high, stringing it toward its next support. Wary of his footing on the eroded narrow road, the congressman took in the panorama. Vargas emerged from behind a large rock. Despite wishing to be alone and undisturbed, the congressman smiled nonetheless at a potential supporter/voter. When he recognized the look on Vargas's face and the danger it implied, his smile faded, replaced by a grimace.

The congressman fumbled with his jacket, an amateurish attempt to draw the pistol holstered in the small of his back. Vargas was upon him quickly, long before the congressman felt the weapon's curved grip, long before he could undo the leather holster's snap. The shove Vargas delivered was hard enough to knock the wind from the congressman's lungs, and certainly hard enough to start him over the precipice.

Vargas savored the shock in his victim's eyes. He saw the spark of realization there, the realization that he would soon be dead. Vargas had seen this look before. He watched as the glaze of coming death replaced the moistness of life. The congressman's sprawled figure became smaller and smaller as it fell, and, when he impacted the sharp rocks, his skull burst. A wet crown of red splattered on the beige dusty stones.

Vargas sighed. Even though his feet remained on terra firma, he too was falling fast.

3: KELPERS

"'Tis very true, my grief lies all within; And these external manners of laments. Are merely shadows to the unseen grief. That swells with silence in the tortured soul..."—William Shakespeare

Prince Albert was jostled awake by turbulence. He looked around the cabin of the chartered British Airways jetliner's cabin. A Special Air Service commando named Major Scott Fagan peered back at Albert with concern. Besides the seat occupied by this hyper-aware bodyguard, the rest of the jetliner's first class cabin was empty. Albert smiled thinly, a signal to Fagan that he was fine. A curtain separated the front of the aircraft from the rest of the cabin.

Beyond this partition sat the others in Albert's entourage, mostly well-connected journalists and government officials. Despite Albert's request, the rest of his army unit suffered the confines and slung canvas seats of a Royal Air Force C-17 Globemaster III, so the jetliner was mainly empty. Albert detected the smell of fresh brewed coffee.

His ears were clogged. As people began fishing carry-ons from overhead compartments, the clicks of the latches sounded distant to him, and the background drone of the airplane's engines was muffled. In an attempt to clear his ears, Albert pinched his nose and puffed up his cheeks. Then he felt a change in air pressure. The aircraft had begun its initial descent. *We must be close to our destination*, Albert surmised. He lifted the window shade, the blinding sun making him wince. It reminded him he had drunk too much the night before. The wispy clouds parted, and the green outline of an island appeared upon the vast blue ocean.

'Speedbird 926'—the air traffic control call-sign of the Prince's flight—emerged from a thick cloud bank that had settled over North Falkland Sound. The flight crossed the north coast of West Falkland at Pebble Island. Passengers pressed faces to the small, oval portals to survey the peak of Mount Adam and the town in its shadow: Hill Cove. Turning east over King George Bay, Speedbird 926 stepped down in altitude. It then banked over the scrubby island and broke over Falkland Sound, the waterway that separated the two main islands. Squinting through his headache, Albert recognized the geography of East Falkland, as well as locales from the Falklands War: Fanning Head, where 3 Special Boat Service had cleared Argentine positions; and, Goose Green and Darwin, where 2nd Battalion, Parachute Regiment had retaken the area from a large and well-equipped Argentine task force.

The aircraft banked low over Grantham Sound and along the Sussex Mountains, then pointed its nose at distant Mount Challenger and flew past Top Malo where a skirmish had been fought between elements of 3 Commando Brigade and determined Argentine Special Forces. On the horizon was Stanley—the capital of the Falkland Islands—and the airport where the Prince's flight would land. He heard the distinctive whine of extending flaps, and a bang and suction as the landing gear lowered.

The British Airways jet floated in over Stanley Harbour. Albert saw the crossed runways that comprised Royal Air Force Base Mount Pleasant. Eurofighter Typhoons—sleek twin-engined, canard-delta wing, multirole fighter aircraft—were parked at the military airfield. There were Apache helicopters as well, one of which belonged to Donnan and Albert. This made Albert think of his mate who was being shuttled along with others aboard the giant military transport. 'Flying steerage class,' is what Donnan had called it. Albert missed the verdant British Isles—especially after the desolation of Afghanistan—so, even the grasslands of the Falklands felt welcoming. Vortices streamed off the wingtips of Speedbird 926 as it lined up with the single east-west runway of Port Stanley Airport.

The ground reached up. The airliner flared before gently settling upon the black asphalt. The tires screeched. The occupants heard the muffled scream of reversing turbo-jets followed by the squeal of brakes. The jetliner slowed and taxied toward the terminal.

Cabin pressure equalized with sea level and the flight crew opened the cockpit windows and poked two flags out: that of the United Kingdom—the 'Union Jack'—and the Prince's coat-of-arms. When they stopped rolling and the engines shutdown, Albert stood and straightened his tired body.

The cabin door yawned open. Cold, salty air blasted inside, bringing droplets from the drizzly grey day. Albert felt the damp in his bones and, surprisingly, missed the dry furnace of Afghanistan. An attendant deployed an umbrella and held it over Albert as he stepped on to the truck-mounted staircase that had 'FIGAS'—Falkland Islands Government Air Service—painted on its ramped side.

A cheer erupted from the waiting crowd, and small Union Jacks waved frantically. Albert rendered a smile. A ceremonial guard stood in formation at the bottom of the stairs. At rigid attention, they formed a gauntlet that led to several waiting vehicles. A military band struggled to be heard above the howling wind.

◊◊◊◊

Despite inclement weather, Albert rode in a convertible and waved to loyal subjects. In the other vehicles—mostly armored Land Rovers—heavily-armed men comprised the motorcade's security detail. The procession made its way along Ross Road on Stanley's waterfront.

Young girls screamed like at a Beatles concert, old men saluted, and, among the throng, Argentine eyes took note. The vehicles rolled by Christ Church Cathedral and Whalebone Arch, passed Victory Green, and then on toward Government House where Albert would be welcomed by, and become a guest of, Governor Roger Moody.

The motorcade turned from Ross Road and onto the shady grove of Government House Road. Albert saw the whitewashed stone mansion where he would stay.

Perched on a small hilltop, Government House stood over a manicured lawn where cloud shadows, caught in the erratic wind, played their ways across the grounds. It had big windows that looked out over the sea, staring as though waiting for a love's return. The mansion's northern façade was dominated by a conservatory, and tall brick chimneys poked from its green-grey roof. Smoke from warming fires floated from their caps before being caught and carried away by the stiff and ever-present breeze. Built in 1845 and home to all London-appointed governors since, Government House stood watch over Stanley Harbour.

Albert sat cradled in an overstuffed wing chair next to a roaring fire that warmed him. A butler stood by to refill the Prince's heavy crystal tumbler with whiskey. Depression and jet lag had combined to exhaust Albert. He felt sleep was upon him. The drink was slipping from his relaxed clutches. A pop from the walls awakened Albert with a spasm. The old building cooled in the evening. Its bones—beams and joists—had been crafted from parts of whaling ships that used to ply the rich waters around the Falklands. They made sounds as if they were still being stretched and twisted by the sea.

"Your Royal Highness," Governor Moody said as he entered the mansion's library. Albert stood up and wobbled. Embarrassed, the governor gestured him down. It was the governor, after all, who should stand in the Prince's presence. However, Albert knew the thin and tall governor to be a combat veteran of the Falklands War, and paid him this respect nonetheless. "Thank you, Your Royal Highness," the governor acknowledged the gesture and took the seat next to Albert. He also accepted a drink from the hovering butler, then removed a fine Havana from a humidor box, lit it, and used a remote to start the stereo.

Chopin's 'Raindrop' prelude began to serenade. Cigar smoke drifted in curls, and then was sucked up the chimney by the convective fire.

Although Governor Moody had met the Prince's motorcade upon its arrival at Government House, he had immediately retreated to the building beside the mansion, the so-called 'wireless room' that housed equipment that kept the remote island in touch with London by satellite. "Excuse my absence, Your Royal Highness," the governor said. "Since the War, we must report in every evening, even when distinguished company is in the House." Distant and mesmerized by the flickering fire, Albert nodded acknowledgment and drank a long quaff from his glass. The governor looked the young man over, recognized his distant stare, and felt equal parts sympathy and reverence for his sovereign. The governor swirled the golden whiskey around his glass, took a sip, and decided not to fill the silence with idle chat. Both men peered at the fire. Among the flames, Albert saw the little girl and the outline of her teddy-bear. The governor, too, saw his own ghosts there, and decided to speak instead: "I think you will find your chambers most comfortable, Your Royal Highness."

"Please, governor, call me Albert."

"Very well. Are you thinking of the war? Of Afghanistan?"

Just as the old warrior had intended with his insightful question, Albert was forced to meet the governor's eyes. "Your Royal Highness…Albert. Though no disfigurement may be apparent, war can wound a man deeply. It is something that one cannot understand unless they have been through the trial themselves." Albert looked over the governor's sharp-featured face, studied the liver spots that made a map of his face, and then peered into his blue, unrevealing eyes. Albert recognized practiced blankness in them, and realized knew pain lurked just below.

"Yes," Albert uttered, with a trembling voice.

"It can be hard for an Englishman to admit this pain, let alone express it. It is not our way. It must be even more difficult for someone in your position, someone with such expectations put upon him," the governor said. Albert wanted to say something, but was afraid his voice would crack if he spoke. Albert felt his throat tighten and tears began to well. "While we are welcomed home with praise and parades, it is often just an ear we need. Someone to listen," the governor continued, took another drink, and peered at Albert over the rim of his tilted glass.

In that moment, Albert realized how much he longed for a relationship with his own father. He also understood how hard it would be for such words to come from the King's mouth, hard for reasons of culture, station, and personality. Hatred of his father was pushed aside just a bit, though the space was readily filled by Albert's self-loathing. Feeling detached from his own life, as though he had stepped out of a movie and had just returned, Albert thought, *I killed a little girl.* The thought became a trembling statement that echoed in his flight–clogged ears: "I killed a little girl," Albert said out loud.

The governor was taken aback. He had assumed the Prince had killed, been forced to kill by circumstance, but he never expected such a confession. Questioning if he had actually spoken the words, Albert added stutteringly: "We targeted a vehicle, dispatched a missile, and a child got in the way." The last words were choked, and Albert began to sob. It was the first time since Jugroom Fort that he had cried. The first time, in fact, that he had cried since he was just a boy. The governor dismissed the butler, moved to Albert, and wrapped an arm around the young Prince.

"It was an accident. Such things happen in war. You were doing your duty, for King and Country." The words only made Albert cry harder. With streaming eyes clenched shut, Albert saw the girl engulfed in flames, a look of surprise and pain on her face.

Albert questioned his own sanity, and, regardless of the answer, realized he would never be the same. The innocence and the carefree days of youth were now an unfamiliar memory. He fought to regain composure. He had contemplated suicide since Afghanistan. That night, by the fire of Government House, with the kind governor's arm about him, Albert promised himself and God he would do no such thing. He would live with the pain. Crying made him realize this pain could be diminished somewhat, forgotten a little, that he could heal. However, Albert was certain that when God decided to take him, he would likely welcome the day.

"Son, I too have killed," the governor said. "Although my rifle claimed many, what haunts me to this day was one night at Many Branch Point. I had thrown what I thought was my last grenade at a retreating Argie. It turned out to be white phosphorous. So, instead of exploding and killing him, it ignited his uniform. He was burning alive. And I was out of ammunition and could not end his suffering. He was just a conscript. Just a boy. He should have been picking up birds in the local café, not aiming a rifle at me and my mates. He cried for his mother as he burned. To this very day, I feel this grief." The governor let out a deep, tormented sigh. "I have become more at peace with the memory, though the nightly visits never seem to stop. Despite this, despite the horrific burdens we carry, we must carry on. As Churchill said: 'If you're going through hell, keep going.'"

That vaunted name stopped what was left of Albert's tears. He sat upright again. Exhaustion had broken Albert's mantle, and he felt ashamed for it happening in front of a stranger, a dignitary he was meant to impress. The governor recognized this.

"Do not be embarrassed. We are all just men. This little chat is between you and me. You have my word as a gentleman."

"Thank you," Albert sputtered, chugging the last of his whiskey. "I think I will turn in"

"This way, Your Royal Highness," the governor gestured to an old staircase.

"Albert, Governor. You may call me Albert. After all, we are all just men," he said with a forced sleepy smile. Filled with respect for the young Prince, the governor watched Albert shamble up the old creaking stairs. He signaled the butler to follow.

Albert's upper floor bedroom awaited, cozy and warm. Modest in décor, it had a wood-fired stove that radiated heat and a soft glow. As the butler retreated, Albert slid under the soft bed's thick duvet. Swaddled in comfort, he peered out a small window to the black sea. On the horizon was the flicker of a ship's deck lights. With his head sinking into the soft, cool pillow, Albert surmised that the lights likely belonged to a cruise ship filled with eco-tourists returning from the Southern Ocean. He fell asleep.

4: WAYLAY

"We're surrounded. That simplifies the problem."—
Chesty Puller

The rotor blades of the Apache thumped and turned
slowly. The helicopter floated along the meadow. Its belly
brushed tall, swaying grass. Ahead were the thatched roofs
of simple houses. Horses scattered and ran away over the
hills.

Albert was at the machine's control. Relaxed, he
looked up through the cockpit glass at the bright stars of the
clear night, then down to his co-pilot's helmet. The man in
front of him never seemed to answer any questions. One of
the house doors opened. Light spilled out into the dark
night, and, one by one, children emerged and lined up
against the brick wall.

The helicopter's cannon rattled and flashed. The children fell in exaggerated spinning deaths. Albert screamed. The co-pilot turned, and, beneath black empty eye sockets, a skeletal jaw hinged open in a mocking silent shriek. Albert screamed again.

"Your Royal Highness. You were screaming." Government House's butler stood in the door frame. His face, shadowed by hall light, betrayed his concern. Albert was drenched in sweat. Major Fagan, now in his fatigues and a beige beret that covered his salt and pepper hair, peeked around the corner. Albert recognized the SAS's cap badge. It was Excalibur. The longsword was pointed down, wreathed in flames, and worked into the cloth of a Crusader shield. Beneath was the motto, 'Who Dares Wins.'

"You all right, then, Captain?" Fagan asked with his thick Yorkshire accent

"Yes, yes, I'm fine." Albert answered. "Thank you."

"Very well, sir."

The butler said he would fetch a glass of water, and he shut the door. The room was swallowed by darkness again.

Suddenly, came muffled thumping, and Albert had to ask himself if he was really awake. Then, hurried footfalls in the hall. Albert swung his legs out of bed. His bare feet hit the cold floor and confirmed he was in fact awake. He clicked the nightstand light on. The muffled thumps became the crackle of gunfire. Albert looked out the window and saw flashes on the mansion's lawn.

"Captain Talbot." The chamber's door was thrown open again. Fagan leaned in, pistol in hand. "Come quickly." Still fogged by alcohol, jet lag, and sleep, Albert sat slumped at the edge of his bed. *"Now,* sir."

The order blasted away the last of the fog in Albert's mind. He complied and moved toward the voice. Seeing he was only dressed in pajamas, Fagan threw a Kevlar vest at Albert.

"Put this on and follow me."

Crouched, Albert and Fagan moved along the House's upper hall. A grenade exploded downstairs. The mansion shook. The blast was answered by a string of automatic gunfire and shouts. Someone was coming up the stairs, too. Major Fagan knelt and raised his SIG Sauer handgun.

"Don't shoot," a voice said. It was Governor Moody and he had an Uzi submachine gun in hand. "Albert, are you all right?"

"So far," Albert answered as he looked over his pajamas and body armor. "What's happening?"

"I'm not certain. The security detail and the mansion guard have failed to answer their radios. Someone yelling orders in Spanish tried to get inside the House."

There was a flash and explosion outside. The three men flinched and dropped down.

"We have to get the Prince from here," the governor insisted to Major Fagan. To my office," the governor insisted.

The three men headed down a narrow set of stairs.

The butler was dead. He lay there at the bottom riser, a shattered glass of water at his side. Albert, Fagan, and the governor stepped over him. Out of respect, each was careful not to contact the corpse. They entered the kitchen.

The simple kitchen held baskets of vegetables, trays of eggs, and, hanging from an iron rack above the hearth, well-used pots and pans. Beside the wood chopping block lay a dead footman. Albert, the governor, and Fagan turned for the lower hall.

They passed a dead dark-haired man folded over a chair. The corpse's uniform was blood-stained and full of holes made by the governor's Uzi. Major Fagan grabbed a handful of hair and rolled the stiffening body off the chair's back. Even though there was no recognizable insignia on the uniform, Fagan declared him an 'Argie.'

Numb and seemingly indifferent to the mayhem, the governor said: "My office is that way." He pointed in the direction of a set of double doors with the barrel of his Uzi. The three moved that way and came upon a hall cabinet.

"One moment," the governor said. They all paused at the piece of furniture. As the governor removed a key from his robe pocket and unlocked the cabinet, Fagan tracked his semi-automatic pistol around, watching for threats. The governor grabbed a shotgun from inside the cabinet and handed it to Albert.

"I trust you know how to use this?"

Albert's answer was communicated by a check of the 12-gauge's chamber. Finding it empty, he cycled the shotgun's forearm and dragged a shell into the chamber.

"Very well," the governor approved.

The three men moved on through the dark smoke-filled hall. The crackle of intermittent gunfire continued outside.

Heavy bootfalls boomed along the upstairs hall. The three men looked up. The sounds stopped at what was the Prince's chamber.

"Carry on," Governor Moody urged. He unlocked and pushed open the door to his office.

The room was empty and undisturbed. A portrait of Captain John McBride hung on the paneled walls, and a large oak desk sat flanked by two tall bookcases that held leather-bound tomes. The governor began clearing books from shelves.

"Lock the door," the governor ordered and Fagan complied. The governor removed the plank of one shelf and pried off a false back, opening into a cobweb-filled crawlspace. "This will get us to the garage. In you go. Both of you." There was no arguing with the diplomat-warrior.

Albert moved to enter, but Fagan held him back and went in first. With Albert and the governor behind him, Fagan felt his way in the pitch-black. He swatted at the sticky webs that stuck to his face and shuffled forward, feeling his way along the lath and plaster. Then he saw light that outlined a small door. He kicked it open and squeezed through.

Albert emerged next to a toppled pile of paint cans that had concealed the door within the garage workshop. Fagan scanned the room. There were tables, racks of tools, and garden implements. He signaled Albert, who emerged, followed by the governor and his Uzi. The governor used his key to unlock the workshop door and opened it just a crack. He peeked through to the garage proper.

"All clear," the governor proclaimed.

Albert and Fagan followed him to the garage where two Land Rovers were parked. The glow of fire flickered through the small windows lining the top of the garage's door. *The mansion is burning,* the fact hit Albert. Again, using the key, the governor opened a wall-mounted lock-box. He removed a key FOB that would start one of the vehicles.

"I'll drive," Governor Moody declared. As the governor knew the roads, neither Albert nor Fagan argued.

93

They piled into the Land Rover. Major Fagan took the governor's Uzi, slapped in a fresh magazine, and handed Albert his nine-millimeter pistol.

"You get in back and stay down," Fagan instructed Albert. With pistol in his dominant hand and the shotgun cupped in the other, Albert rolled over the rear seat and into the back of the Land Rover.

The governor started the vehicle and opened the garage door with a remote that hung on the shade. As the door rose slowly, the governor revved the engine.

Impatient with the slow door he yelled: "Sod it," and reversed out, splintering the edge of the wooden portal. He spun the Land Rover around in the driveway, rocking its boxy body, and squealed its wide knobby tires.

Small arms fire plinked off the armored vehicle's sides as the last of the enemy assault force had turned its fire from the mansion guards to the escaping Land Rover.

Through a gun-port in the Land Rover's door, Fagan sprayed bullets back at the offenders.

"We must get the Prince to Mount Pleasant," the governor said as they sped away. He glanced at the burning mansion in the rearview mirror, and passed a fire truck racing there. The Land Rover's engine revved and shifted through gears as they accelerated. "Anyone want some air? It is a bit stuffy in here," the governor said with utter calmness. Albert and the soldier shared a smile of mutual admiration for the rock-steady governor.

The Land Rover's wheels screeched as the governor turned past '1982 Liberation Monument' and Thatcher Drive, and then onto Reservoir Road.

"Look out," Albert yelled as they almost smashed into an ambulance pulling out of King Edward VII Memorial Hospital. They zoomed by Scotia House Bed & Breakfast where tourists had emerged to gawk at the raging fire at Government House. Darting through light traffic, they passed residences on the left, and the Community School and Library on the right, and then a satellite dish that Argentine guerillas had wrecked, by driving a delivery truck through the small complex's perimeter fence

"London has no idea, do they?" Fagan asked.

The governor and Albert stole a glance at one another. Now on Darwin Road and quickly leaving the urban area of Stanley behind, the road narrowed and its surface changed from asphalt to loose gravel.

The Land Rover's big tires and heavy weight came into their own, biting in and keeping the vehicle stable. With much of the city's lights extinguished, it was easy to see the night aglow with scattered fires. Each illuminated rising columns of smoke. The three men stared ahead in silence.

In the vehicle's squinted headlights, the road narrowed further, and, edged by drainage ditches, threatened to grab the wheels of the speeding Land Rover. Winding among hillocks, the vehicle began to rock back and forth as the governor skillfully followed Darwin Road. Albert looked out through the big rectangle frame of the rear window.

Two bright dots appeared in the tail of dust that the Land Rover left in its wake.

"Governor?" Albert mumbled.

"Yes, I know. We're being followed."

The governor stepped on the accelerator. The Land Rover lowered and pitched forward as more horsepower was put to the road. There was tapping at the Land Rover's side and windows. What they first thought was kicked up gravel was in fact small arms fire.

Fagan grabbed the shotgun and opened a side window. Cool sea air blasted inside. He leaned out, and, with successive booms that made Albert's ears ring, emptied the shotgun at their pursuer. Behind them, the bright headlights swerved.

Fagan chucked the empty shotgun to the front passenger seat.

"Uzi, please," he requested. Albert handed him the square, stubby submachine gun. Fagan fired. Ejected cartridges clinked against the window as he emptied the magazine with a ripping sound. In the rear-view mirror, the governor saw tracer rounds trail off like laser beams. They sparked as they impacted the front of the pursuing vehicle. The chasing headlights swerved again. Then they tumbled one over the other as the pursuers crashed. One light flickered and extinguished as the wrecked vehicle came to rest upside down.

"Bastards," Fagan yelled into the night, then leaned back in and kissed the stock of the Israeli-made weapon.

The speeding Land Rover went airborne as they topped a small hill. Zooming down the other side, they saw a big fire raging in the distance.

"That's at the airport," the governor concluded. A trail of fire shot across the sky. It reached from offshore and toward where the fire was already burning. A new fireball bloomed as it impacted the ground. "The airport is being pummeled."

Fagan picked up binoculars and looked to sea, where a merchantman sat at anchor. It was a container ship, its decks covered by multi-colored forty-foot steel boxes, the kind that electronics and spare parts are shipped in. Except these seemed to contain surface-to-surface missiles.

Fagan watched as the top of a container lifted. A missile tilted up on its launcher and ignited. It slid off its rail and arced into the sky and at the island. *Club-K Container Missile System*, Major Fagan realized, recognizing the Russian weapon from an intelligence briefing. He panned his view over to Stanley's dock.

At the dock, a small cruise ship was berthed. Men in uniform disembarked and made their way inland.

"My God, it's a full-scale invasion," Fagan said.

A shockwave shook the Land Rover. In the distance, a fireball mushroomed as it rose.

"That was the fuel tank farm at Mare Harbour," the infuriated governor said. He had considered the attack on Government House as a terrorist attack, with potential perpetrators ranging from the IRA to Al-Qaeda, but it was now obvious that this was much more.

In stunned silence, Albert, Fagan, and Governor Moody sped along Darwin Road and toward the Royal Air Force Base at Mount Pleasant.

"The radio," the governor realized. "In the glove compartment." Fagan fumbled it open and revealed the small transmitter/receiver. He pawed at the microphone, stretched the coiled wire, and clicked the transmit button.

"Any station, any station, this is Major Scott Fagan, 22 SAS Regiment, over." A warbling static was all they heard over the speaker. "There's jamming."

"Try again," the governor advised.

"RAF Mount Pleasant, RAF Mount Pleasant, we are inbound with a special package. On Darwin Road, light-green Land Rover, diplomatic plates, over." For a moment, they heard a response in English, though it was cut off by high-pitched interference. Then, briefly, there was Spanish.

"Culebra dos zero dos, tratando--"

A searchlight appeared. It reflected off the calm dark waters of Bluff Cove.

"What's this then?" Albert huffed.

The armed scout helicopter announced its arrival with bright yellow flashes and a burst of fire from its slung machine gun pods.

"Bollocks," the governor shouted.

The Land Rover swerved and leaned precariously as geysers of dust erupted along the roadside. The silhouette of the enemy helicopter flashed again, and the sound of its three-bladed rotor hacked at the night. Albert studied the aircraft's silhouette as the governor did his best to avoid the bullets that impacted around them.

"That's a Chinese Z-11. Twelve-point-seven-millimeter guns," Albert recognized.

"Our armor cannot stop that big a round," the governor said. He yanked the wheel over. The Land Rover left the confines of the road, bouncing hard. Albert hit his head against the roof. The governor swerved the Land Rover through the wet grass and mud as he tried to make it a difficult target. They rounded a boulder dropped eons ago by a receding glacier. On the other side was a vehicle full of men.

One had a rocket tube on his shoulder. There was a blinding bright flash, and the governor skidded to a halt, but the missile streaked over them. Albert, the governor, and the major ducked and braced as an explosion rocked the Land Rover. Turning around, they saw the helicopter, swallowed by fire, fold in half and drop to the rocky ground. Bits of earth and rock pitter-pattered on the vehicle roof. In the Land Rover's headlights, they recognized the men as Royal Marines.

"Hurrah," the governor shouted.

They approached the main gate of Mount Pleasant air force base. Beyond the fence-line, at the end of the base's runway, sat a wrecked jetliner. Firefighting foam surrounded its scorched fuselage, and smoke curled from where its ceiling had burned through. The governor recognized the jetliner's tail markings as belonging to the Chilean national airline, though the jet seemed to be an older model, one that did not belong to this airline's modern fleet. Then Governor Moody remembered his war-game briefings: enemy special forces would land by ship and aircraft, likely commercial ones using distress calls to open otherwise closed doors. In the case of RAF Mount Pleasant, it was apparent the attempt had failed. Beyond the wreckage was a big yellow bulldozer that had been parked on the runway. Moved there in haste, it had sheared the jetliner's landing gear, ripped open its belly, and caused it to crash and burn.

Fagan pointed out several other smoking piles of metal on the airfield's apron, and saw one of the base's fire trucks spraying what appeared to be a destroyed helicopter.

Despite the inferno it had suffered, Albert recognized its form as belonging to an Apache. He wondered if it had been his loyal machine.

Led by the marines, the Land Rover approached the main gate's sandbagged heavy machine gun positions. A guard signaled them to halt, and, with his pistol brandished, approached the vehicle.

"Hello," Albert said to the stunned officer.

"Blimey," was all the man could say. He signaled for support. Several others jogged up carrying their SA80 carbines. Albert got out and was encircled, a shield of flesh and steel formed around him.

"The governor," Albert insisted. The governor abandoned the vehicle and joined the Prince in the middle of the circle. "I owe you my life," Albert shook his hand.

"A life certainly worth living," the governor said with a smile. Albert nodded acknowledgement. With Major

Fagan in tow, they all moved inside the base's perimeter and to the main building. Once there they were introduced to a very busy looking officer, Mount Pleasant's commander.

"There is a transport waiting on the tarmac. As soon as we clear that wreckage," the base commander said, pointing out a window to the burnt-out jetliner, "We will have you on your way."

"What's that all about?" Fagan queried.

"An airliner transmitted a mayday—claimed engine trouble—and we cleared it for an emergency landing. Then all hell broke loose. When we realized what was happening, I had heavy equipment driven out, and the tower warned them off. As you see, they did not heed this warning. The airliner landed smack on top of a bulldozer. The enemy assault force was consumed while strapped in their seats," the commander said. Although he was glad his men did not have to contend with them, he nonetheless felt sadness for the means of their demise.

"Which of our aircraft survived the attack?" Albert asked.

"One Typhoon and a few helicopters. Luckily, the C-17 was safe in the maintenance hangar and under guard. Infiltrators got the rest." He pounded his fist. "They managed to take out the satellite link. So, I doubt London even knows what is going on."

"Infiltrators?" the governor asked.

"Locals. They had worked on-base for years. One of them was a fuel bowser driver, and at least one was a trusted mechanic. They set explosives, and one crashed a jeep into the Blindfire radar unit at the west end of the facility. Without it, our Rapier surface-to-air missile battery is all but useless."

"Fiends," Fagan kicked in.

"But it was not just locals," the base commander continued. "The airliner was full of Argentinian soldiers. We have one survivor in the infirmary with horrible burns."

"And the Apaches?" Albert asked.

"Two survived; were saved."

Having not flown since the attack on Jugroom Fort, and certain he would never fly in battle again, Albert could not believe his next words: "Get me in one."

"What?"

"We have to get you out of here; off the island. You cannot go gallivanting about a warzone," the governor said.

"I'm a pilot in His Majesty's Army, and once you wear the uniform, you're part of the game. Service to our country will always come first," Albert affirmed.

"You are the Crown Prince. If anything should happen to you..." the governor worried.

"I have cousins. They can rest their bottoms on the bleeding throne. Get me to an Apache, now."

"Look, I'm your superior officer, and I order you to stand down. I will not take responsibility for such foolishness," the base commander asserted.

"Actually—regardless of rank—as Prince, Captain Talbot has the authority," the governor stated.

"A helicopter, then. And a flight suit," Albert spoke with calm determination.

"Yes, Captain. The machines and some of your men are in the west hangar."

"Then that is where I want to be." Albert turned to the governor and Major Fagan. "Governor Moody, you will get on that transport and as soon as you are beyond the range of enemy jamming, report what you have seen. Tell London we require immediate reinforcement."

The governor only nodded. Torn between departing—leaving his post—and the orders of his sovereign, he reluctantly complied.

Albert, the accompanying marines, and Fagan entered the hangar. Several pilots readied the two Apache attack helicopters that had survived sabotage. Among the men was Lieutenant Bruce.

"Donnan," Albert said with relief.

The big Scotsman beamed back.

5: DRAKE'S DRUM

"Duty is the essence of manhood."—General George S. Patton

Albert got dressed in the hangar storeroom. His hand shook as he lifted the heavy fire-resistant olive drab flight suit. He ran his thumb over the rough embroidery of his Afghanistan campaign patch. His pulse pounded in his temples, and a click reverberated through his skull as he tensed his jawbone and ground his teeth. He had to concentrate to slow his breathing, and he felt a tingling in his extremities. He began to hyperventilate and squeezed his eyes closed. In the pinkish darkness, he saw fire, and the black silhouette of a little girl. Albert shook the image from his mind. Instead, he remembered the governor's words: *It was an accident. Such things happen in war.*

Albert's breathing slowed. *You were doing your duty, for King and Country.* Albert stepped into his flight suit and zipped up. He donned his light blue beret, and tucked his flight helmet under his arm. He mustered his strength and entered the hangar.

Albert came face-to-face with an Apache. He saw his wan reflection in the cockpit glass. The helicopter's belly cannon aimed right at him and the nose ball turret mount looked like a proud chin, jutting from between the cheek avionics bays. Slung from the stub wings he observed four Hellfires, and, on the opposite side, the launcher for CRV7 rockets and a single blue-bodied Stinger air-to-air missile. Albert reached out and touched the Apache's cold metal skin.

He felt an electrical shock when he made contact. It had bitten him like the dangerous animal it was. A technician came around. Albert hoped the man had not

seen the doubt in his eyes, and walked away. As he strode
to the hangar office, he repeated to himself: *Keep calm and
carry on.*

Everyone had assembled in the hangar's office. The
base commander strutted over, a print-out clutched in his
white-knuckled hand.

"Gentlemen, we are left with several machines, and
we are going to use them. Prince Albert has joined our
ranks, and, despite my vehement protests, insists on taking
to the air. Reports are sketchy. Here is what we know: At
0300, Argentina commenced invasion operations. We
believe the opening moves included the seizure of an
offshore oil rig, an attempt to assassinate or capture the
Prince at Government House, bombardment of Stanley
Airport, the landing of troops at Mare Harbour and Stanley,
and what may have been a truck bomb at the marine
barracks. We have also lost feeds from the three mountain-

top radars, and must assume them to be in enemy hands or destroyed. As we all know, enemy commandos also tried to land here at Mount Pleasant. They did not succeed. However, saboteurs were able to destroy all but one of the Typhoons belonging to No. 1435 Flight. They got a Special Air Service EH101 Merlin. Just two of the recently delivered AH Mark 1 Apaches are intact, with one suffering minor damage. The Globemaster is safe, and we will evacuate the wounded and the governor with it. There are no friendly ships close enough to offer immediate assistance. His Majesty's Ship *Iron Duke* left these waters four days ago and is probably half way to Portsmouth by now. As far as we know, we have no submarines in the vicinity. There is no word from the other towns on the islands, and we have been attempting to contact London. Unfortunately, it seems all the satellite relays have been disabled. It is also apparent that at least some operation participants were locals. So, we must assume some of the population is hostile. I would guess Argentina kept the initial invasion forces light to keep us from detecting their build-up, but we must also assume that heavier forces are on the way. With just one Typhoon left in theater, it is obvious that the enemy has air superiority. Regardless, we will use what we have left to challenge this status. Our plan is to defend our base—and by extension the approaches on Darwin Road, and the town of East Cove—as well as harass enemy operations until we receive instructions, are reinforced, or are relieved. Once the runway is clear, the Typhoon will escort the Globemaster out, with an Apache providing perimeter cover. We will keep the second Apache in reserve. We have also formed anti-air teams, armed with Javelins."

A soldier entered the hangar and spoke with the commander. "Excellent. The runway is clear. Right then.

The transport will fly out in ten minutes. Captain Talbot. Lieutenant Bruce. Man your Apache." The base commander turned to the Typhoon pilot. Knowing the man would be going up alone, flying without a wingman for cover, he said: "Captain, to your aircraft."

The C-17 Globemaster III had already lined-up with the runway and held for take-off. Beneath the strategic airlifter's angled wings, four turbo-fans increased power. The Typhoon was already airborne, circling overhead at high altitude. All by its lonesome, it would try to keep enemy fighters off the C-17's back.

Albert hovered the Apache near the base's eastern perimeter fence. He was to handle any enemy anti-air teams that popped-up in the base's surrounds. He scanned the terrain with the Apache's night vision system. The exposed hilltops and wide-open ground would make it easy to spot any threats at a distance. He turned his head to the runway's apron. The C-17's bright strobes flashed and, with brakes released and engines whining, began to roll. Overhead, the Typhoon banked with a scream and "Greyling two-nine, on guard" came over the Apache's radio as the fighter checked in.

Slowly at first, the big transport moved down the runway. Then, belying its size, it accelerated quickly. Donnan and Albert scanned the horizon for trouble. With nothing on their night vision system, they waited as the transport rotated and lumbered into the air. Its navigation and landing gear lights were immediately extinguished. The C-17 tucked its wheels away, and then banked south to avoid trouble.

"Bandits, inbound," the Typhoon pilot reported, his voice strained by the high-G turn he was performing. "I count four. Greyling two-nine: Engaging."

The Typhoon turned into the enemy four-ship. Determined to keep the bad guys as far away from the climbing C-17 as possible, the pilot nudged his throttles past the stop and into afterburner.

Raw fuel dumped into the engines' exhaust, ignited, and kicked the Typhoon past Mach 2. Using its PIRATE—Passive Infra-Red Airborne Tracking Equipment—Greyling 29 recognized the shape of the approaching bandits. Flying triangles with twin streams of hot thrust, the British pilot knew he faced Mirages, a French-built delta-winged supersonic fighter aircraft. The Typhoon pilot looked to his weapon read-out.

Just one Meteor air-to-air missile was on its station, and there were only 300 rounds of 27-millimeter ammunition for the Mauser BK-27 revolver cannon. Looking through the canopy and off to his right, he lamented the fact that no one was on his wing; no friend to protect his six. The sky was awfully dark and the Typhoon was awfully alone. Regardless, Greyling 29's pilot threw the aircraft at his adversaries and closed fast with them.

Donnan tilted the Apache's night vision turret skyward as he attempted to locate the Typhoon. Stars streaked across the cockpit screens. Like comets, they trailed white and green. A solid green line appeared. *Tail-fire...* he thought. *An air-to-air missile.* Morse code-like tracer fire shot from the Typhoon. He witnessed two high-altitude explosions as the Typhoon bested two Mirages.

A big aircraft broke from among high-altitude clouds and rolled inverted. It was painted in tiger-striped greys, and sported the flag of the Argentine Republic high on both of its twin tails. Marked along the fuselage in black letters was: *Fuerza Aérea Argentina.* The aircraft was one of two J-11s in Argentina's inventory, a pirated Chinese copy of the formidable Russian Flanker heavy air superiority fighter, provided to Buenos Aires in kit form as part of an ore-for-hardware counter-trade. At its stick was one of the Argentine Air Force's best: Captain Lucas Moreno. As Moreno began to shed altitude, he kept the radar off to minimize emissions and instead relied upon a small fish-eye lens mounted in his Flanker's canopy.

This infrared search and track system detected and displayed the heat emitted by his enemy, and thus found the British Typhoon as it trailed the last aircraft that belonged to a three-ship flight Argentina had assigned to patrol the block of airspace over the British airbase. When the Typhoon took to the air, they had raced in to engage. The Typhoon—a formidable machine with a skilled pilot at the controls—had, despite numerical disadvantage, turned the tables, and the Argentine Mirages let out a desperate call for backup.

Moreno had swept in from his orbit high above East Falkland. He superimposed the Typhoon's heat signature in the lens's crosshairs and used it to follow. He rolled the Flanker again, nosed it over, and dropped the throttles, using the pull of the earth to shed altitude. Then, Moreno pushed the throttles to the stops, and the Flanker screamed as it dove on Greyling 29.

A high-pitched warble sounded in Moreno's ear. The PL-8 Thunderclap short-range infrared-guided missile on his right wingtip begged for release. Another Chinese-built steal of Russian technology, the missile left its rail when Moreno squeezed the stick's trigger, and, now freed, began to home on the heat generated by the Typhoon's two turbofans.

The British pilot was focused on the last Mirage he trailed. His plane rocked back and forth as he stayed with the Mirage, sending whips of glowing tracer fire its way.

He did not see the Thunderclap as it curled in, and, since the missile tracked passively, his systems offered no warning.

The Thunderclap detonated above the Typhoon. Its blast fragmentation warhead sprayed the Typhoon with shrapnel that tore the rear-half off of the aircraft. The Typhoon's tank, ripped open and spewed its contents, and the fuel ignited in a bright, tumbling fireball.

Albert and Donnan saw the blast on the Apache's screens. They followed the fiery wreckage as it plummeted down to icy Choiseul Sound.

"Hope that's an Argie," Donnan said, though his gut told him otherwise. Besides the thumping rotors, silence otherwise filled the Apache's cockpit. A moment later, the loud quiet was broken by a crackle on the radio.

"Greyling two-nine, Mount Pleasant," the base radioed in vain.

The transmission repeated once again.

Only static replied.

Albert scanned the sky for parachutes, but he spotted none.

"This is British garrison, Port San Carlos, British garrison Port San Carlos, over," the radio hissed. "We're under attack by superior enemy forces; in danger of being overrun. We request any and all immediate assistance."

Donnan turned and looked back at Albert. Albert read the urgency of his co-pilots gaze and, in that moment, decided he would save his countrymen. He would mitigate his guilt with honor and pride.

"Fuel?" Albert queried.

"There's enough." Donnan had read Albert's mind. Albert jerked the Apache into a turn, dipped the nose, and began speeding off toward the west. He looked to his navigational computer.

"GPS signal is weak. Likely being jammed. I'm taking us due west in the direction of the coast. We'll follow Darwin Road, and then move along the shoreline."

"Roger, mate, understood," Donnan seemed eager for redemption as well.

A radio transmission came through. Mount Pleasant begged an answer. The base controllers had seen the Apache's radar blip move from its assigned position and off their screen. Although there would be hell to pay and questions to answer, both men ignored the radio and instead focused on their cockpit instruments.

Flying at 180 miles-per-hour—the helicopter's maximum speed—Albert skirted the Apache over the rocky ground. It was a moonlit blur above the tall grass and rock. Following his compass, Albert swerved the machine to avoid a lone wind-stunted tree that he used as a visual reference. The Apache came upon Darwin Road, intersected, and began to follow it.

The Apache flew over Swan Inlet and its adjacent ponds, and then over Laguna Ronde, Laguna Isla, and Laguna Verde. Its disturbance alighted flocks of kelp gulls from the waters. As the machine screamed overhead, its rotor-wash kicked up a fine spray from the still waters. The terrain this side of West Falkland shot by. It was rippled, squeezed, and molded into parallel undulating hills. The road veered south toward the town of Darwin, but the Apache continued west. The sun began to rise.

The dawn's early light painted Darwin Sound purple. The helicopter reached the coast of the Argentine Sea. Albert banked to follow the cliffs glowing gold in the new light. The cliffs were licked by foam and seaweed-topped breaking waves. The Apache's thumping blades scrambled sea lions from their rookeries, flopping into the cold sea.

The scenery was beautiful and brought a moment of peace to Albert. With the machine's rhythmic vibration and the penetrating warmth brought by the new day, both men felt tiredness settle in. Feeling his eyes drooping, and longing for a hot cup of tea, Albert made conversation.

"How have you been holding up?" he asked Donnan. With these spoken words, Albert immediately felt his concentration and depth perception sharpen, and the hypnotic effect of speeding over white-capped waves diminished.

"I'm all right, mate."

Albert should have known he would get nothing from the rock-of-a-man seated before him. While he full well knew Donnan suffered under the burden of their shared memory, the Scotsman had a way of keeping it in, burying it, drowning it in liquid forgetfulness. A beeping interrupted Albert's thoughts.

"Air search radar off to the left," Donnan read the computer warning.

"Give me a heading," Albert ordered.

"Two-seven-nine."

Albert threw the Apache over onto its side. He pulled away from the shoreline and started out over deeper, darker water.

"Computer has classified the threat radar as a Thales track-while-scan," Donnan announced. On the horizon, a silhouette appeared. It was small and dark-grey; a military vessel.

"Looks like a patrol or guided-missile boat. Definitely not one of ours," Donnan said.

"Yes," Albert grunted. He was focused on piloting. Donnan zoomed in on the target with his imaging system. He scrutinized the contact's profile.

A high mast jutted from the vessel's block of superstructure, topped by a big onion-shaped dome. Then, as the boat turned toward them, a deck gun became discernible.

"Jammer on," Donnan said as he activated systems that would confuse the enemy transmitter. Albert increased speed. "I take it we are engaging?"

"Warm up the Hellfires," was Albert's answer.

"Roger. Longbow spinning up. Hellfires coming online."

The target vessel picked up the Apache's electronic emissions. Realizing it was being tracked, it lofted canisters full of zinc-coated fiberglass chaff. The canisters bloomed over the boat and formed radar-reflecting clouds. Despite the attempted deception, Donnan had already acquired a fix on the target's hull. They saw a puff of smoke from the boat's deck gun. The Apache shook as the shell air-burst just behind and to the side of them.

"Weapons free," Albert declared.

Donnan wasted no time. The Apache bucked with the shift in weight as the missile left its rail and fluttered across the water. Firing and forgetting, Albert broke for the cover of shore.

The Hellfire bounced millimeter-wave radar off the Argentine guided-missile boat. Skittering across the water, the missile zeroed in on the reflections, and flew itself directly at the target's center of mass. Moments later, the Hellfire slammed into the superstructure of ARA *Gómez Roca*.

Most of those on *Gómez Roca*'s bridge died fast as the vessel's superstructure became an abstract flaming metal sculpture. After a secondary explosion, *Gómez Roca* started to roll. In the distance, as the small Argentine vessel began to sink, the black Apache hugged the coast and sped north-west. Albert would use the sharp rocks to hide his radar signature from roving fighters and enemy search radars. The helicopter soon crossed a spit of land.

The Apache broke the spit and sped over Bonners Bay. Pokers Point was off to the left. The aircraft zoomed over Blue Beach British War Cemetery where 14 Falklands War casualties were forever interred. Both Albert and Donnan saluted as they passed over the stark isolated place. Turning north, the Apache raced over heaving ground. It flew on toward a collection of small, white structures astride a harbor.

"There," Donnan said and pointed. He could see Port San Carlos. Immediately apparent were grey vessels tied up at the town's single jetty. Several landing craft had beached themselves past the settlement's breakwater, too.

Smoke rose from the harbor's warehouses. Assault troops swarmed over the area like angry ants. On the hills above, British artillery hammered away. Their tubes flashed and smoked as they rained shells upon the intruders. The enemy fanned out from the harbor and streamed up the hillside. It became obvious that the precarious situation had the British positions in danger of being overrun.

"Sevens," was all Albert said.

Donnan readied the rockets tucked beneath the Apache's wing pod. Per standard tactics, the helicopter would loop around from behind the British defenders and, once the friendlies were safely behind the aircraft, fire at the enemy.

The Apache ripped over the beach, the same beach that, long ago, 2 Para had landed upon. Albert climbed the machine with the terrain, banked the helicopter over North Camp Road, and then back around toward the water. The

Apache came in low over cheering British forces. It dropped, hugged the downward slope of the hill, and its panel light flashed green. The CRV7s were ready for release.

"Igniter circuit open," Donnan announced.

Albert used a fixed reticule to align the Apache's flight path. They sent a salvo of CRV7 rockets on their way. There was a whoosh, bright flashes and trailing blue smoke as the weapons left their launch tubes.

Glowing like fireflies in the dawn, each of the rockets spun for stability and deployed small fins. At a predetermined distance, their outer casing peeled away like banana skins, releasing a cargo of flechettes that formed black clouds of small tungsten darts that dove on and ripped into the Argentine marines.

Donnan added to the chaos on the ground by discharging his Chain Gun. It rattled and Albert felt the

132

Apache yaw. He used the pedals to compensate, nullifying the increased torque with the tail rotor, and kept the Apache straight and level. This gave Donnan a solid platform from which to rake the enemy with fire.

Earth and rock shot up from the ground. Arms splayed and rifles dropped. Men fell face first; their mouths filled with mud. Men choked on the very ground they had wished to conquer.

"Hellfires," Albert ordered as he jinked the Apache's nose toward the enemy boats tied up at the jetty.

A small patrol boat was first to be painted by the laser beam emanating from the Apache's gimbaled nose turret. The three remaining Hellfires ripple fired, and, one after the other, the enemy vessels exploded.

Ammunition on one boat ignited with a torrent of sparks, a pyre of inspiration to the handful of defenders high on the hill. Donnan let out a war-cry and Albert felt a warmth flow through his body. *Perhaps the cure for the guilt of killing*, he thought, *IS MORE KILLING*.

Albert giggled. Not the giggle of a happy child, but a twisted, burdened giggle that would frighten anyone who heard it. A radar warning sounded, interrupting his rapture.

Albert squinted and saw a small helicopter that had raced to the scene. It had a diminutive silhouette when viewed head-on.

"Is that a Cobra?" Albert asked Donnan. He believed it to be a US-built attack helicopter.

"Negative. Too small."

"'Kay…Stinger. Shove it up his ass," Albert ordered the air-to-air missile made ready.

"Roger," Donnan acknowledge with a snort-of-a-laugh.

Tracer rounds zinged around them.

Albert cursed the small machine that dared to challenge them.

He loosed the Stinger.

The little missile's smoke trail zigzagged away as it centered on the Argentine *Aguilucho* (Harrier) attack helicopter.

The Stinger found its target and swallowed it in a fireball, spitting out little metal bits that splashed into the water with boils of white foam.

This kill represented Albert and Donnan's first air-to-air encounter; the cockpit restraints kept them from bouncing with excitement in their seats. Albert pulled the Apache into a climb. His half-baked plan was to loop around again and dive on the enemy as they clawed their way up the hill. With nose-up attitude, the Apache reached the apex of its turn. There occurred a deafening blast.

The Apache was slammed sideways. Donnan hit his head against the canopy frame. Albert lost his grip on the cyclic control. The Apache rolled on its side and began to fall. Cockpit lights flashed. A whooping sound told of damage to vital systems. Albert fought to right his spinning aircraft.

They were hit again. This time, sparks cascaded from an overhead panel, and smoke announced a fire that had erupted in one of the engines.

Deep thuds.

This meant the helicopter had absorbed more hits. However, with the crew compartment and electronic bays swaddled in Kevlar blankets, Albert and Donnan were kept alive. The Apache: stayed airborne.

"Aircraft at six o'clock high." Donnan had spotted their prosecutor: a big twin-engine fighter.

"Flanker?" Albert recognized the silhouette from training, although he had not expected such an aircraft type in-theater.

Seeing smoke pouring from the British helicopter, Captain Moreno peeled off. He was satisfied he had a kill, and he finally heeded his fuel level warning.

Albert watched RPMs in both engines fall off. Oil pressure indicators had pinned at zero.

"Goddamnit," Albert spat. "Auto-rotating."

Around them, the Apache died.

Albert dropped the collective and nosed the aircraft over as he disengaged power to the main rotor. Using airspeed to control rate of descent, he pointed the helicopter at Falkland Sound.

"I think we can make the opposite shoreline," Albert said as he fought to control the power-off glide. The Apache fought back. Albert chose the landmark of

Chancho Point as an aim point, and worked hard to keep the rocky peninsula in the windscreen. The tail rotor bled off energy. The Apache, unable to fight the torque, began a flat spin.

Donnan reached up to brace against the rise in G-forces. With hydraulics failing, it took all of Albert's strength to manipulate the flight controls.

He grunted against the strain. The world outside spun faster and faster and became a smudge of blue and brown. Donnan closed his eyes to fight off vertigo, and Albert leaned against the cockpit wall to brace against the rotation. Every time the blue of water became the brown of land, Albert nudged his crippled Apache in that direction.

Land is better than water, his mind rationalized as it clung to consciousness. If they hit water and were knocked out, the Apache would sink like a stone and neither would escape. Albert adjusted collective pitch to increase the

138

driving region of his rotor. The descent slowed. Albert judged that they were near sea-level. He spotted the streaked brown of solid ground and raised the collective. The rotor stalled and the machine dropped hard.

A jarring crunch…

And blackness.

6: WHITE DOVE, WHITE HARE

"Sometimes even to live is an act of courage."—Lucius Annaeus Seneca

Afraid to see the little girl's burnt blood-covered face, clot-caked hair, and judgmental coal-black eyes, Albert tried to turn away. Despite the attempt, he could not, however, and as usual, he was forced to behold the horror. She was a shadow at first. Then, for a moment, she became aglow with freckled pale skin and long blonde curls. Her eyes flashed bright blue. They were piercing and welled with sadness.

"Wake up," she whispered. "You have to help me."

◊◊◊◊

Albert gasped as he awakened. Fumes and ozone burned his nose and throat. He coughed. The wrecked

Apache hissed and smoked. Its fluids leaked. An arcing electrical panel sparked and zapped in the cockpit. Albert moved achingly, his vision clearing. Donnan was slumped and did not move.

Albert realized Donnan's helmet was cracked. Blood streamed from the torn opening. Albert tried to raise his own head. Sharp pain forbade it.

"Donnan," he mumbled. The toxic air made him cough again, his breaths poisoned by the slow-burn of materials that made up the cockpit interior.

Albert released the harness. While the movement was minor, it sent him spinning with vertigo. He threw up on himself. Covered in a cold sweat, Albert fought to move within the cockpit chair. He lifted himself from its confines. On the verge of falling unconscious, he slumped back again. *Concussion.* Albert worried about Donnan; he still had not moved.

"Donnan," Albert repeated. The he tried yelling: "Lieutenant Bruce."

The stabbing pain in his head told Albert not to do that again. He groaned as he tried to keep himself from vomiting again, or, worse, from blacking out. It would be up to him to get out and retrieve Donnan. Albert reached for the Apache's canopy release.

The mechanism's red handle required more strength than Albert could summon. He fished a knife from his flight suit pocket and used its shiny blade as a lever, working the canopy release until it clicked free. Then, with dizzying effort, he rotated the release to the 'Unlock' position.

The canopy lifted a few inches. Fresh salty air flushed the cockpit. Its warmth blew away the chemical-laden fumes from within. Albert's head cleared, and his thoughts became less disjointed.

"Donnan. Wake the hell up."

Only seabird song answered, accompanied by the howl from wind forcing its way into the cockpit. An acrid smoky smell came in, too. Albert turned and saw the column of black smoke rising above the crash site, emanating from one of the engine pods. He did not, however, see nor smell the fuel that had leaked out of the punctured tank.

Albert strained his aching neck to look past his other shoulder. He saw that the Apache had broken in two; just where its tail boom had struck a big, immovable boulder. He looked up and saw that one of the helicopter's composite rotors had snapped, too, and only the thin titanium strip at the leading edge held the blade's frayed carbon fibers. His head movements did not bring spinning, confirming his vertigo had passed. With a grunt, he raised his arm to press a hand against the canopy glass.

Pushing hard, Albert coaxed the canopy open a little bit more. This provided enough room for his aching body to squirm in the seat. He pushed himself up and, with his shoulder, pressed against the canopy. The canopy budged and creaked up to a new position. There was now a big enough space to crawl through. The wind entered full-force and delivered salty spray that refreshed Albert's sweaty face. This provided the inspiration he needed to get free.

Albert attempted to lift his legs out, but managed only to hook his ankles over the metal lip of the cockpit's threshold. *Progress*, he thought, and shimmied his calves over the edge. Pushing with his arms, he launched his torso upward until he felt the sharp metal in his gut. Fighting nausea, Albert rolled and let gravity do its thing.

He grunted as he hit the ground. The jagged rock that poked Albert's side told him to focus. He rolled onto his back. The grass felt soft and cool against his face, and the morning sky: baby blue. Albert spied a fluffy cloud and focused on its abstract shape. He found an elephant there, and remembered how he and his brother Henry would lie on the lush lawns of Balmoral and find such puff-forms. He suddenly missed his big brother—a feeling he had not had in ages—and muttered his name: "Henry." His big brother could not help him anymore, though, so Albert did his best to lift his body and stand.

He managed to get to a crouched position and paused to fight the urge to throw-up again. His concussed brain spun with vertigo. Albert rubbed the big, black, knotted bruise on his forehead, and fell back into the tall, swaying grass. He lay beside the wrecked Apache that cradled the body of his closest friend. Albert heard nothing but his own deep breathing and fell asleep.

The sun began to burn Albert's face. His lips were dry and cracking. He awakened with a groan and lifted his throbbing head. He looked to his broken helicopter.

Grey smoke rose from the Apache's engine pod. It feathered on the wind and painted a trail in the sky that led right back to the crash site. Albert felt a sudden urgency to get away from the area. He saw that Donnan was still slumped in his harness. Albert knew his co-pilot/gunner—his friend—had died. Albert rolled onto his side and sat up. The world turned fast. He propped himself on the one arm that was not sore, and stood. He wobbled and leaned against the Apache's bent fuselage and felt his way to Donnan's side.

The blood from Donnan's head wound formed a black pool of coagulated ooze. Albert reached for his friend's jugular and searched for evidence of life. The skin was cold and rubbery, and there was no telltale pulse.

Donnan was free; had no more guilt or worries. Albert unclipped Donnan's harness. He would lift the body out when he could muster the strength. For now, though, he just reached for the radio that still had power despite evidence of shorting. He tuned the radio's dial over to an emergency frequency and clicked transmit.

"Any British forces, any British forces, this is an army attack helicopter. We are down, and require rescue, over." Careful not to give his call sign or location, Albert waited a moment before repeating the transmission. There was nothing. Not even static. Albert turned his attention to Donnan.

"Okay, mate," he said to his lifeless friend, and with a heave, pulled the body from the cockpit. Donnan's foggy eyes seemed to look right into Albert's own eyes. Their dull glaze frightened him. Donnan's eyes had always displayed the glint of happiness and intelligence in them;

had always shown his good soul in the black pits of his pupils. Although the brightness had faded a bit after Jugroom, his gaze always comforted Albert, and was full of life. Now, Albert could see, Donnan was truly gone, someplace far off, or, perhaps, nowhere at all. Albert had a sudden renewed love of being alive, and he felt very selfish for his long courting of dark thoughts. The certainty filled him that a man like Donnan could not be in Hell, that God could not judge a brave and upright person for one mistaken night on the battlefield. Calm settled over Albert.

In that calm, a voice told him there was a purpose for everything. Even the worst days of life were precious, that they made us who we were, taught us lessons when we needed them, and reminded us of what was important. Albert even felt it possible that the nameless little girl who had perished at their hand had forgiven. That she, too, was free of the bounds of earth, of the hard mud floor she had slept on, the scant food and filthy water she had swallowed, and the dirty, torn clothes she had worn. Most of all, she was free of the men who had not cared for her, who had loved killing more than they did their little girl, and who had caressed the cold gun-metal of a Kalashnikov instead of her smooth, warm face.

Sudden anger swamped such thoughts—anger at any father who could put ideology and death above the greatest gift God—any supposed God—could give: a precious child. Albert realized he must forgive himself. Even as a bird in a gilded cage, and handed the life-sentence of being a royal, there were those who were worse off and lived their own private hell. That moment, Albert realized, he needed to grow up.

"Sorry," Albert whispered into Donnan's ear. Albert lifted and folded Donnan over his shoulder. He took a few steps before he had to lower the big man to the ground. He dragged Donnan close to the cliff edge from where his friend could look over Falkland Sound. It would be a good place for his friend to rest until British forces could repatriate the body, or, perhaps, should his parents wish it, have him laid to rest within the British military cemeteries on the islands. Albert took a deep breath of cool air. Or, even remain forever in its place, he pondered. The wind whipped at his cheeks. He closed his eyes and turned toward the sun. His face collected its warmth. *You are alive*, Albert thought. Then, he began to collect rocks.

Even though he was still dizzy, Albert felt better. He sat for a moment to listen to the howl of the wind and the waves that crashing against the cliffs. He leaned over the side and watched as the waves obliterated themselves against the rock and then reached up the cliff with foamy fingers. He smiled. He was, after all and despite his supposed or imagined importance, inconsequential in the scheme of things. This realization made Albert happy, if for just a moment. He lifted one of the rocks he had collected and studied it. It had been around for millions of years, a piece of mountain beaten down by wind and rain, broken off by the sea, and delivered to this field. *I am inconsequential.* This made things simpler. He looked to Donnan.

Albert laid his friend out. He folded Donnan's arms over his chest like an entombed pharaoh, and carefully placed on top the stones he had collected. As Albert piled them, he pondered: *He, too, began as a mountain of greatness, was tempered and shaped by the wind of life, cracked into smaller pieces, and he would finally become a grain of sand on an endless beach.* Albert placed a final rock, and then stabbed a stick into the pile. He balanced Donnan's cracked helmet upon it.

Albert stood over the grave for several minutes. He pocketed the items he had collected, items that would identify the body: a Velcro patch with LT. D. BRUCE from Donnan's flight suit, as well as the dog-tags that hung from his neck. Albert rubbed the dog-tags. He felt the raised letters and numbers. He clicked his thumbnail on the small notch used to jam the tags between a corpse's front teeth for identification purposes. If Albert could get off this island alive, he would personally deliver these small things to Donnan's closest relative. With duty to his comrade complete for the moment, Albert shifted his focus.

Evening came fast. Albert would need a place to shelter and inventory his supplies. Before this, however, he had one more duty to one other fallen comrade: his loyal mount.

Broken, Albert thought. *My sweet machine is broken.* Albert opened an electronics bay on the cheek of the

Apache's fuselage. *I am sorry.* He lodged a grenade within, and then pulled the pin before retreating to the protection of a boulder, to await the explosion. A few seconds later, it happened, though the sound was muffled by the gusting wind. Black smoke rose from the helicopter's electronics' compartment, and Albert felt assured that the sensitive communication and other classified components would not fall into enemy hands. However, he felt as though he had just punched an old friend. Albert rubbed his eyes with exhaustion and stood again.

The smoke from the helicopter's engine pod had finally stopped its spewing. Albert spotted the holes where the enemy's bullets had ripped through the Apache's armored skin and destroyed its vital systems: electronic, hydraulic, and mechanical. He felt lucky and amazed that he had been able to nurse the helicopter down in one piece,

154

and that he had survived. *A gift. From whom?* He wondered. Then he reminded himself that Donnan had not been so lucky. *Donnan…* Albert ran his fingers over the jagged edge of one of the bullet holes. The torn metal cut his fingertip, and he realized he had been lucky that the enemy fighter did not turn in to deliver a strafing run—a coup de grâce—on the crash site. Albert looked around for a place to hunker down.

He found a small grotto at the top of a cliff that provided some protection from the blast of wind. Albert shimmied inside, sat on a relatively flat shelf of rock, and emptied his supplies from his rucksack. Among the collection, he examined two knives, two Glock 17 pistols with extra magazines with several boxes of nine-millimeter ammunition and three L109A1 anti-personnel grenades. Non-combat supplies included a compass, several foil packets of drinking water, a small bottle with a built-in filter, a first-aid kit that included packets of quick-clot to slow hemorrhaging, a sewing kit, several MREs—meals ready-to-eat—some tins of biscuits, a signal mirror, and a signal flare. He also examined a small pair of binoculars; a foil heat-retaining blanket; a Bible, Koran and Torah bound in a single miniature book; a notebook for keeping a journal; an inflatable splint that doubled as a pillow; a packet of five cigarettes; some waterproof matches; and a bar of phosphorous to start a fire in any weather. He finally noted a card with the Royal Army's coat-of-arms on one side and a request for proper treatment of the bearer under the terms of the Geneva Convention on the other. Albert chuckled when he saw this request was written in—besides his native English—Arabic, Farsi, and Pashtu; an obvious leftover from Afghanistan and Iraq.

Albert opened one tin of biscuits and a packet of water. When he was done eating and drinking, he began to inflate the splint/pillow. Each puffed breath reminded him of the mild concussion he had suffered. He spread the foil blanket across the rough floor and lay upon it. Resting his head on the pillow, the events of the last few days played in his head like a newscast. As the sun began to set, golden light pierced his grotto and illuminated the dust he had kicked up. Albert fell fast asleep.

Thumping echoed in the grotto, the sound entering Albert's restless dreams. Awake now, Albert felt the sound in his chest. He looked outside.

The stars still sparkled, and the night air was cold. *Helicopter*, Albert realized, and tried to discern the blade-count among the repeating noise. He decided he was hearing a two-bladed machine, though the echo made the direction of approach difficult to ascertain. With the prospect of being rescued, Albert got up and went to the grotto's entrance. The sound drew closer and a spotlight glinted off the sea that surged below. Caution quickly replaced excitement, slowing his actions. Albert checked that the magazine was well seated in the handgun, and then racked the slide, chambering a round. He crawled to the grotto entrance. He squeezed against the rocks, and peeked to where the Apache was sprawled over the ground. A helicopter burst from behind the opposite cliff-face.

Albert recognized it as UH-1 Iroquois…the ubiquitous 'Huey' of American origin. The Huey swept its spotlight. The bright oval moved over the ground, paused at Donnan's grave, and then washed over the Apache, fixing its stare to study the crash site. The yellowish eye then began to scan the nearby terrain. Albert fought the urge to run out and declare his presence with waving arms. Then he spotted a light-blue and white roundel on the helicopter's side. *Argentinians…*

Albert ducked back into his hideout. The enemy aircraft flew about, and then it chopped hard at the air and settled to a hover. Albert placed the second Glock and grenades on a rock near the grotto opening. *They can knock*, he thought, looking at his meager weaponry, *but they cannot come in*. The sound of the helicopter changed as it configured for landing; the sonic booms at its rotor tips becoming sharp and loud. *They will be on the ground in any moment*, Albert realized.

Albert needed to see what he was dealing with. He placed a grenade in one of his flight suit's many pockets, drew his primary pistol again, and crawled a few feet outside. Sneakily, he peeked from between two pillars of rock.

The Huey landed near the Apache and several uniformed men emerged from the cabin door. As they deployed, Albert recognized the soldier's weapons as FN

FAL battle rifles, completely outgunning Albert and his little Glock. An Argentine officer jumped out. He had a submachine gun slung from his shoulder. Pivoting and pointing, he directed his men to spread out and search. Then, frighteningly, he seemed to look straight at Albert. A hot, prickly rush shot throughout Albert's body. He ducked behind the rock and held his pistol close. He caught his breath, and, looking again, saw he had not yet been spotted.

Major Ezequiel Vargas swept his flashlight around the wreck of the downed British helicopter. He walked as his subordinates ran about. Vargas stopped at Donnan's grave and lifted the cracked flight helmet off the stick. Looking inside, he read the owner's name: Lt. D. Bruce written on a piece of masking tape; a mark Albert had not been aware of, and had neglected to find and remove. Vargas knew this name, had heard it in an intelligence brief.

He also knew with whom this particular co-pilot/gunner had shared the helicopter.

"Albert Talbot," Vargas snickered. "Crown Prince of the United Kingdom."

As a member of the forces that had occupied Argentinian land and killed Argentinian sons, Albert was Vargas's chief quarry for the campaign. That the Prince was on *Las Islas Malvinas* proved that Argentine preparations for war had gone unnoticed, that their deceptions had worked, and that the British considered another attempt to seize the islands by force as highly unlikely. Capturing the Prince would be Vargas's royal prize, the ultimate leverage, a tool of barter worth the return of *Las Islas Malvinas* to the republic once-and-for-all. However, Vargas's mission did not include desecration of graves. He was, after all, a soldier. Carefully, Vargas returned the British pilot's helmet to its perch. One of his team approached and reported.

"*Mayor, no se encontró ninguna señal de el piloto.*" There was no sign of the pilot that had obviously survived the crash.

"*Extenderse,*" Vargas ordered his men to spread out.

Vargas spotted a boot print in the dirt. His trained eyes then scanned a circle around it. He saw a pressed tuft of grass where a man had lain. Vargas moved to it and crouched. He looked for the next telltale, and found it in a rock that had been kicked over, moved from the depression within which it had sat for hundreds, if not thousands, of years. Vargas picked up the rock. He lifted his flashlight beam to float over a nearby crag. *Defensible, protected from the wind. That is where I would be,* Vargas thought. He signaled to two of his men, who ran over. Vargas swung his Star Z-84 submachine gun up to cover the two

Argentinians advanced toward the cliff.

"Shit," Albert muttered. He could feel the approach

of an enemy in the primitive stem of his brain. The

fatigued, though otherwise rational part of his mind,

wondered wishfully if Argentine prisoner camps were as

famous for steak as the rest of the country. He chuckled

mirthlessly. He looked to his pistol, and then to the

grenades. He had an idea.

Albert found a small slab of rock, placed it in the

entrance to the grotto, and wedged a grenade beneath it. He

pulled the pin, but made sure to keep the weapon's safety

lever from springing. He quietly collected his items and

placed them in the rucksack. As he did so, he carefully

avoided his little trap. He scurried out of the hole.

Wrapped in pitch-black night, Albert made his way along the cliff, away from where he heard pursuing footfalls. He balanced along a spit of rock and tucked into a vertical crevasse. There was a flash and a bang.

Albert peeked around the lip of rock. He saw smoke billow from the grotto. Two enemy soldiers had thrown in a grenade that would stun anybody inside, and with a nod to Vargas and then one another, stormed the grotto. A muffled explosion told everybody there that they had triggered Albert's grenade trap. Within the confined grotto, the over-pressure and shrapnel had been lethal. Outside, Vargas swore and waved away the resultant smoke. He waited a moment and then entered. The slaughter he saw within was evident on his face when he reemerged. Frustrated, Vargas looked around. This time he caught sight of Albert's head. Summoned by the explosion, other soldiers had arrived, too.

Clinging precariously to the cliff wall, Albert fought against his concussion-diminished balance. The rocky beach was not far below. So, when Albert lost his footing and grip on the nearly sheer cliff-face, he fell backward onto his rucksack.

The impact forced the air from his lungs. Albert gasped to replace it. He rolled against the cliff-base and slid beneath an overhang. He lay in the wet sand, caught his breath there, and then rolled over and up to flee. Flashlights danced on the beach around him. One blob of light settled where Albert's body had left an impression in the pebbles. From above, came urgent shouts in Spanish. Shards of spalled rock began to fall around Albert. *They're coming down*, he realized.

When he heard voices near, Albert, pistol at the ready, gathered his courage, and stepped out. Aiming up the cliff, he saw three forms rappelling down ropes. The gun barked as he emptied it. Having sent 17 bullets in just a few seconds, he managed to mortally wound two pursuers. One man fell to a pointed rock, the crack sickening Albert. The other dangled from the rope that had caught his ankle, and swung dead in the wind. Before Albert rolled back under the protective space, he caught Vargas's cold gaze.

Vargas pointed at Albert. That jabbing digit said: 'I recognize you; You are mine.' Albert's heart pounded from adrenalin. His hand shook when he tried to seat a fresh magazine in the pistol's well. He finally found the space in the grip, smacked the plastic magazine home, and released the slide, chambering the first round. Albert felt his chest pocket. The bulge and weight of a grenade was evident. He heard the helicopter again. Its engine whined as it spun up and increased power for take-off. Albert tried to remember if he had seen any armament on the aircraft. Regardless, he decided he had better find cover.

An eerie silence enveloped the area. For a fleeting moment, Albert thought that the helicopter had departed the area, and sped off in another direction, but a roar washed this notion away, and the Argentine Huey dropped along the cliff-line. It dipped its bulbous nose toward where Albert had squeezed into a crack. It screamed in, and came parallel to Albert's position.

Albert saw the flashes from the open cabin door. He heard the ricochet of the bullets that impacted around him, and swore aloud as he tried to stuff himself further into the folds of rock. He heard a blast from above. Albert craned his neck to see the source of the deafening sound. And then, another blast, making his ears ring. He saw smoke erupt from the helicopter's engine pod and red lights flashing on its cockpit panel. Pilot silhouettes played their controls as they nursed the Huey's single Lycoming turbo-shaft engine.

As a helicopter pilot, Albert could see the movements as frantic. Most pilot movements were controlled and fluid. However, these shadows moved with an air of panic. The smoke and human iterations said the machine had been injured. The Huey bucked as its problems were compounded by failing systems. The shadows in its cabin grabbed handholds. When stable, they shifted the aim point of their rifles. No longer focused on Albert, they were instead trained on the cliff-top. One of the rifles flashed. Albert heard the supersonic zing of a bullet travelling overhead. *They're no longer shooting at me*, he thought. Another form in the Huey's cabin smacked the head of the rifleman who had fired. The shooting ceased.

There was another bang from the top of the cliff, and another hole appeared in the side of the Argentine helicopter. Oil spurted from this wound like dark blood. Pushed by the rotor wash, the vital oil ran in streaks down the side of the engine cowling. More red lights flashed on the Huey's cockpit panels. The men who pulled its strings knew when to save themselves; when enough was enough. The Argentine helicopter banked and raced off along the cliff. As it retreated over the black sea and above the din of waves and the whip of wind, Albert heard a scream of victory. The voice that delivered it was of a higher pitch. It belonged to a woman. When the gusts subsided for a moment, Albert heard the voice again.

"You can come out now," she shouted.

Wiggling his jammed ankle free, Albert crawled from his hide. He moved out on a small ledge and saw the silhouette of his savior. She was petite and had long hair that tossed about in the air that rushed up the cliff. The curls shifted left and then right as the breeze changed direction. Her rifle—a .303 British by the look of it—was almost as long as she was tall. Holstering his sidearm and slinging his rucksack over his shoulder, Albert began the climb to meet his savior. He pulled himself over the cliff's lip and stood up straight before her.

"Aethelinda Jones. You can call me Linda," she said. Then Linda squinted. Her flashlight blinded Albert as it moved about his face. It paused at his eyes and mouth. Both had a shape she recognized. "Do I know you?" she questioned, but she already knew the answer. Then her mouth opened in amazement. "My Goodness," she said, shocked. She knelt.

"Please," Albert pleaded. He took her hand and tugged her back up.

"Were...were you in that helicopter that went down?" she stuttered. Albert caught a glimpse of Linda's freckled pale skin and big green eyes in the flickering flashlight.

"Yes," Albert said. "I think we should turn this off for now." He felt her shaking hand and clicked off the flashlight. "Thank you. You saved my life. You could have been killed, you know?" he said.

Linda shrugged.

Albert looked out to the water and the silhouette of the retreating helicopter. He was thankful they had ceased firing on a woman, even one blasting away with a big bore hunting rifle. Albert touched her gun's long, blued barrel, and admitted: "Nice."

"I have had it since I was a little girl. My father taught me to shoot as soon as I was strong enough. You must be hungry. And tired. Come. Let's go," Linda Jones insisted.

At the small family farm, the sheep enjoyed more living space than the people did. Albert saw a cottage that beckoned with a rope of smoke, rising from its chimney pipe, but the weathered barn was at least three times its size. The cottage had smallish windows that glowed yellow and warm, and a moss-covered stone roof that would keep those within dry and cozy. Albert and Linda walked along a mud path by a short stone wall. They passed the barn and the sheep that bleated within.

They rounded a hillock blanketed by a fragrant flowerbed. Like the flowers, the cottage's walls seemed to sprout from the very earth; growing as living rock reaching up for the stars. They moved on to the cottage's heavy oaken door and the heavy wrought-iron knocker that hung at its center. The door flew open. Albert flinched, and his hand instinctively went to the butt of his holstered pistol. However, when he saw the old man with the shotgun, he managed to stay his hand. The old man inquired gruffly, "Who goes there?"

"Easy, Dad. We have a special guest," Linda proclaimed. A herding dog—marbled black and white—ran from the house, barking wildly at Albert.

"Eight ball…" Hearing Linda say his name, the dog stopped barking, flapped his tongue out, and panted with a seeming smile. Then, with a halo of light about her, a little girl stepped into the cottage's doorframe. She clung shyly to her grandfather's leg. Albert froze. He shifted his weight as he examined the familiar vision. His feet seemed caught in the suction of the muddy ground. *I know you*, he thought. He had seen this little one before. The scene had been a vague fleeting image that hid in the folds of his memory. But now it had suddenly sprung to his conscious mind like a bolt of electricity.

"Hello," the child whispered shyly.

"Prince Albert, this is Anne, my daughter," Linda said. "And this is my father, Henry.

"Prince?" Henry questioned. "Yeah. And I'm the bleeding Pope."

"Dad, try not to be so rude always." She turned back to Albert and her face softened. Then back to her daughter and father. "Anne. Father. This is Prince Albert." Linda performed an exaggerated curtsy with a crooked smile upon her face. Anne batted her eyes and blushed.

Linda recognized her daughter's instant fondness. The glow in her daughter's eyes spoke of the tales of knights, towers, and dragons. It was, after all, not every day that a sheep shearer's daughter met a real live Prince.

"How do you do?" Albert greeted the old man. Then he crouched and looked at the little girl who squirmed at her grandfather's side. "Good evening, Lady Anne," Albert said to Anne.

"Please, Prince Albert, do come in," Linda signaled.

"Albert. Please, just call me Albert."

"Albert," Linda giggled as if the privilege of familiarity tickled her. "Please," she added, and gestured for the open door. "*Dad*." Linda's bossy tone got her father to lower the twin barrels of his shotgun. This petite farm girl was obviously in charge.

Albert entered the small cottage, feeling like he had travelled to some parallel universe. The cottage was far more spacious than its modest exterior had implied, and, he saw, the decorations were traditional English. The first thing he noticed was the hutch that displayed blue and white plates. Although not the finest of China, each plate, nevertheless, showed off attractions of Great Britain.

The images were a tourist's menagerie; A mail-order variety of places. Each reminded someone of the place where they belonged. A place beyond sheep pastures, endless empty grasslands, and cold unforgiving seas. Albert took in the collection: There was the Iron Bridge of

175

Shropshire, Hadrian's Wall, Stonehenge, Kings College, and the Blackpool Tower. Finally, on an oval serving plate, framed by three panels, were Buckingham Palace, Balmoral, and Windsor Castles. Albert grinned and looked over the furniture.

The chairs and sofa, all shrouded by blankets, were brightly-colored and hand-knitted with local wool. They likely hid the furniture's tatters and holes that came from years of comfortable use. One of the chairs was draped in a grey and white blanket. However, this particular blanket opened one yellow eye, and turned out to be a very fat, very old cat named Grey Bear. Awakened, Grey Bear gave a quivered stretch. With half-closed eyes, he 'sussed up' Albert, and decided it was not worth moving. He circled in place and collapsed again. Absorbing heat from the small fireplace, Grey Bear drifted off to sleep again. Albert smiled and continued to look around.

The sitting room's wallpaper was faded and busy, and most of the paintings that hung there could have been done by the numbers. Albert rubbed his eyes. Then he spotted one piece in the collection that caught his interest. It had sail boats moored off a grass marsh, and, on a beach, a couple shared a picnic beneath an umbrella as a child made castles in the sand. Albert leaned in to get a closer look. He saw from the signature that Linda was the artist.

"This is quite good," he said. "I can see you're a fan of impressionism."

Linda smiled gratefully. Had she been born elsewhere—away from the farm, perhaps in a city like London—Linda would have been an artist. Her attic was crammed full of pieces she felt unworthy of display. Although many were gems that could populate an exhibit, they had long been banished to collect dust and cobwebs, reminders of a life that could have been, but never came to be. Linda looked to her dry callused hands, and thought: *Not the hands of a painter.* Albert rubbed his tired itchy eyes again.

"Tea?" Linda offered.

"That would be lovely, thank you." A nice hot cup was just what Albert needed.

Ten minutes later, Linda had set the table for a 'smoko,' a traditional Falkland serving of tea and toast usually reserved for mid-morning. She had even boiled a fresh egg for the weary Prince.

"Hope you don't mind sheep's milk," she said as she poured it into his cup.

"Not at all," he said, and thanked her.

Linda offered Albert a slice of thick grain bread and set out an assortment of preserves and honey. "All from the garden," she added with a smile. There was a long quiet moment as both Albert and Linda sipped from their cups.

"Annie," Linda belted, jarring Albert from his tranquility. The delivery of the child's name was enough to chase the little girl from where she had been peering between the banister rails and back to bed.

They detected heavy breathing from the living room. Henry was sound asleep again in his favorite chair. Its worn fabric and overstuffed pillows embraced his skinny body. Albert smiled and had another sip. He found the tea quite aromatic, dark, and hot, and it washed down the chewy bread nicely. "The butter is so sweet, is it not?" Linda queried. Albert hummed contentedly in answer. "Our only cow spends all day chewing grass and eating my flowers."

"It's delicious," Albert declared. He had not tasted anything this good in some time. "The honey...it tastes of rapsflower blossom."

"It's pale maiden, actually. The bees love them," Linda added thankfully with a smile. "When you're done, I'll find you some clothes. My Dad made up a bed for you, as well." She saw worry spread over Albert's face and read his thoughts. "Will they come after us?"

"Yes," Albert spoke bluntly. "I should not linger."

"We can care for ourselves," she looked to the rifle propped beside the door, and then to the shotgun at her father's feet. His gasping snore made them both laugh.

"I need to make my way back to base; back to Mount Pleasant."

"I know a few fellows that may be able to help."

"Your husband? Anne's father?" Albert took advantage of the opening to find out more about his savior and host.

Linda did not answer. She just shook her head. Albert understood that her husband, whoever he was, was gone. From her expression, Albert also surmised the man had passed away.

"I'm sorry," Albert offered uncomfortably, and took another bite of jam-smeared toast as he stirred his tea. She removed the tea cozy she had knitted, tipped the pot, and filled his cup again. When Albert sat back and rubbed his belly, Linda pointed the way upstairs.

In order to avoid waking Annie or her father, Albert and Linda were both careful to tread lightly when they climbed the creaky stairs. Linda guided the way to her bedroom. There was mostly silence as she went through the drawers of her husband's dresser. She held articles of clothing up to Albert to judge their size against his body. Albert could see sadness and loneliness in the emeralds of her moist eyes. As she held a wool sweater over his torso, their gaze met and held. Albert wanted to kiss her, and suspected she would welcome it.

"This looks like it should do," she turned away with a blush. "You are a little taller--" Linda sighed instead of finishing her sentence. "Well, then. Off to bed with you." She pointed to the room just down the hall.

Albert peeled the smelly flight suit from his sticky skin, and crawled between the cool, soft, clean sheets. He stashed his Glock beneath the deep, fluffy pillow, lay his head down, and fell deep asleep.

Albert awakened to serene morning light streaming through lace curtains. However, a worrisome pounding at the cottage door jarred him. He bolted from bed and down the stairs.

7: ARAPUCHA

"Guerrilla war is a kind of war waged by the few but dependent on the support of many."—B. H. Liddell Hart

"Quickly; in here," Henry said, as he gestured toward an opening in the floor. The thunderous rapping at the door became even more insistent and was accompanied by yelled Spanish.

"No. Where is your shotgun?" Albert countered as the Glock in his hand would not suffice against an enemy breech team.

"Don't be daft. Leave this to me. We need you to stay alive and out of enemy hands. Now, do as I say," Henry left little room for argument.

Albert began to climb down into the hide. He paused on the rickety ladder.

"Where's Annie and Linda?"

"Tending the herd," Henry answered and pushed down on the top of Albert's head. The hatch closed and he was swallowed by the pitch black of the old root cellar. Albert heard the carpet being dragged back over the hatch. He shivered.

The cottage door splintered. The soldier with the battering ram stepped aside to allow his armed comrades to enter in a practiced fluid motion. Once inside, they formed a semi-circle around the immovable Henry. Each soldier—Argentinian flags on their shoulders—pointed their assault rifles at his chest. Vargas strolled in, pistol in hand. Henry saw something unsettling in the cold stare of Vargas's dark brown eyes. *This one would kill without hesitation*, Henry knew, and he swallowed hard.

In the black of the root cellar, the sounds of creaking boards and stomping boots echoed, and dust from the creaking floorboards overhead rained down upon him. Muffled voices, and then a stubborn shout from Henry: "God save the King." As the last syllable of the old man's battle cry was enunciated, Albert heard a single pistol shot, followed by the thud of Henry's body as it collapsed to the floor. Albert was filled with equal parts fear and rage. He heard footsteps climb the staircase to the second floor of the cottage. When the sounds retreated, and Albert heard an engine turning over outside, he got up on the ladder and pressed his shoulder against the hide's hatch door. With some effort, he raised it enough to roll Henry off, and peeked through.

Albert felt like a rat leaving a nest. He had hid while an old man stood his ground. As he scampered out, Albert resolved to never again accept sacrifice in the name of his position. He looked to Henry. Blood streamed from his mouth and nose, and there was a single red hole torn in his chest. While barely alive, he locked eyes with Albert, and, with a painful last breath, muttered, "Annie. Linda. Tell them I--" Albert closed the man's eyelids and finished the sentence on his behalf:

"Love them. I will tell them, sir."

Albert decided he would find Annie and Linda before the Argentinians did. With his rucksack, Henry's shotgun slung over his shoulder, the Glock in its holster, and Linda's .303 in hand, Albert ran from the cottage to the barn. He tried not to slip in the mud and manure as he made his way, and he then spotted the sheep trail that snaked up to the pastures beyond a rocky crag. He hiked that way.

Albert saw the herd wandering aimlessly in the pasture as Eight-ball the dog lay dead upon a grassy gnoll. Annie and Linda were not to be seen, though two muddy ruts told Albert that a truck had been there.

Someone yelled from behind him, and Albert turned towards the cluster of rocks. Several men stood with rifles pointed his way.

"Lay down your weapons," the man with a grey beard, tweed jacket, and cockeyed hunting cap commanded in English. Though the accent was like nothing Albert had heard before, it was certainly British English. Albert lowered his rifle.

"Annie…and Linda Jones?" Albert huffed, exasperated by their absence and unknown fate.

"Who are you?" grey beard asked.

"Captain Albert Talbot. We have to find them."

"Talbot? Albert Talbot."

"Prince Albert Talbot?" Grey beard's scowl became squinted as he studied Albert's face.

"They cannot be far," Albert urged.

"Far enough. But we will catch up, don't you worry. Captain Talbot, I am Gubbins. This is McGregor," he pointed to another. McGregor was a stick of a man decked out in plaid flannel; "Calvert," the young blonde-haired man nodded; "Fairbairn," this one looked gin-soaked with a web of blue veins tattooing his face and red nose; "and Sykes," this last man was a six-foot-four pile of muscle with just a hint of moustache. "We're 'The Warrahs.' Partisans. Like in '82, we will fight until no foreign soldier walks our land." Albert looked them over. Other than young Sykes, the men looked like they belonged in a pub recounting old tales over a pint, not walking about a combat zone. Albert decided, however, he would not underestimate them, or judge them by their age or looks.

Pleasure," was all Albert could say as he took a moment to soak it all in, feeling weak in the knees.

"Captain Talbot," Gubbins said: "I believe you are now in command." Gubbins looked over Albert's civilian clothes. "Last I read you were in Afghanistan, am I right?"

"Yes. I'm a pilot. I fly a helicopter."

"What are you doing out here?" Gubbins asked. Albert did not answer. Gubbins smirked, and added: "Shot down, then, eh?"

"Linda saved me," Albert said and surveyed the grasslands. He was eager to follow the trail.

"Yes. She called this morning. She told me everything. Sounds like you owe her a debt."

"I do. I have to get her and Annie back. Then I need to get to Mount Pleasant."

"We need to check on Henry—Linda's father—at the farm. Then we'll help you get back to your base."

"He's dead," Albert shook his head.

The men looked sad. Then they got angry.

"Right, then. So long as we kill as many Argies as we can along the way, we are with you." The men acknowledged his statement with nods and grunts.

"Do we need to bow before you?" Fairbairn asked sarcastically.

Albert shook his head, and, to deflect talk of his status, asked: "What is a Warrah?"

"It's an animal. A cunning and ferocious fox native to the islands," Styles replied. Albert liked the answer.

"We have a truck at my farm, It's the next one over," McGregor offered.

Keeping within the hollows of hills and among the folds of land, Albert and his new-found mates set out for McGregor's house.

An old pick-up truck pulled a trailer full of hay along the road, winding between boulders jutting from the grass.

McGregor drove. The truck rounded another hillock and slowed when a road obstruction became visible.

"Checkpoint," McGregor mumbled with disdain.

The Argentinians had set up a series of crates to slow approaching vehicles and force them to weave among them. A tent had been set up beside the road and a troop truck with a pintle-mounted machine gun watched over all. A soldier manned the weapon and swept it toward the pick-up as it drove his way. Immediately, when they saw the approach of the old truck, other soldiers that manned the position snubbed out cigarettes and raised rifles to the ready. McGregor passed a red and white sign that ordered '*HALTO*;' stop in Spanish. He pressed the brake pedal. The brakes squeaked, and the old truck coughed and threatened to stall.

"*Buenos dias, señor,*" the soldier greeted McGregor when he lowered the truck window. McGregor nodded hello. *"Papeles*. Uh…papers." McGregor fished out his vehicle permit, his license, and his passport. The man examined them and asked: *"¿A donde vas*? Where are you going?"

"To a sheep farm outside Darwin. I have a load of hay for them." McGregor gestured back toward the trailer he hauled. The soldier signaled one of the men to check the load. McGregor shifted in his seat.

"You must pay a fee to use this road: 50 pounds sterling," the Argentinian said as he leaned back into the truck's window.

"Sterling? I have only Falkland Pounds. Anyway, I've already paid for this road. Every year I pay for this bloody road. It is called, 'taxes,' mate."

"You paid those to the occupiers, to London. From now on, you will pay your liberators in Buenos Aires. Today, *señor*, you will simply pay me." McGregor wanted to draw the Beretta .380 hidden at his side and put a bullet between the eyes of 'his liberator.' Instead, McGregor smiled and stole a peek at the side-view mirrors. He saw a soldier take out a knife and begin to stab the bales of hay stacked on the trailer.

"*¿Señor?*"

"Yes, yes, I will pay," McGregor declared and looked into the rear-view mirror.

"Yes, I know you will. Or, I will be forced to seize your vehicle and trailer."

The soldier probing the hay caught the tip of his knife on something.

"*Jefe,*" he called out to his superior. "*Algo esta adentro.*"

"You have something inside your hay?" the soldier asked McGregor. "*Por favor*, you will step out now, *señor.*"

McGregor shuffled across the seat, and used the cover of his motion to grab the pistol. He swung it up and fired a shot at the chest of the soldier. With that gunshot, the trailer's hay bales erupted. Automatic fire sprayed from within. Like a jack-in-the-box wound to its limit, Sykes popped out the top. He immediately chucked a grenade into the bed of the Argentine troop truck. The resultant explosion lifted the soldier up and out, and splayed him on the cracked blacktop. The Warrahs' truck began to roll again, and, before Sykes closed the wood and chicken wire-framed hay hide, Albert peeked out.

The Argentine troop truck was on fire and dead enemy soldiers were scattered in a circle. The truck sputtered and drove off, its trailer of hay in tow.

A familiar Huey helicopter came over the hill, hugging the ground. Its rotor chopped the moist air, and pushed the ground fog away in swirls. Even though the Huey still had the holes Linda had made with her rifle, it had been repaired inside. A man leaned out from the aircraft's cabin. He braced himself against the door and pointed when he saw the checkpoint, the very one that had failed to respond to headquarters' radio calls.

Vargas tuned to his pilot and yelled above the whine of the Huey's engine: "*Ayi estan.*"

Vargas's gunship circled the area in a wide arc. The gun that pointed out of its cabin declared ownership of the area within which all were subject to prosecution.

"*Estan muertos,*" one of Vargas's team noted the obvious: Everyone at the checkpoint was dead. The Huey's pilot hovered over the adjacent field, and then set the helicopter down on its tubular skids. Blades of soft green grass were pressed beneath their hard steel.

Soldiers exited the aircraft and fanned out. They knelt and brought rifles up to their shoulders. One by one, Vargas went to each of the checkpoint's dead Argentinians. He felt their necks for a beat. Finding none, he became ever more angry and frustrated. He got on his radio to request a new detachment of men to collect the bodies, and take over the position. This miserable dirt road, barely noted on most maps, had become the escape route of his game. Clenching his teeth, Vargas spotted and picked up bits of hay scattered along the roadside. He twirled his hand in the air and his men pulled back to the Huey, jumped in, and, hanging their legs from the cabin, took to the air again.

"*Vamos a saltar encima de ellos*," Vargas told the pilot, and pointed off to the south-east. He and his men would leapfrog Prince Albert and his compatriots.

◊◊◊◊

Kicking up stones, The Warrahs truck drove along the bumpy dirt road. McGregor fought the steering wheel to keep the trailer from going into the drainage ditch. Gubbins sat beside him with Albert and the rest of the men hidden in the trailer. They crested a hill. A sprawling horse farm lay ahead and below.

The farm included a long stable and a huge barn beside a big white house. Almost a serene scene, MacGregor realized there were no horses in the fenced paddocks. Gubbins pointed out a clump of what looked like camouflage netting. From beneath this innocent plant-like charade jutted four dark missiles pointing skyward.

"Surface-to-air missiles," Gubbins said.

Muddy brown ruts dirtied the farm's otherwise bright green field, leading to and from the emplacement. Several vehicles—troop trucks and jeeps—were parked just inside the open barn's doors, and soldiers milled about. Apparently, the horse farm had become a center of enemy activity.

"That's John Nelson's farm. Hope the old boy is alright," McGregor said to Gubbins.

The road passed close to the farm's periphery and ran along a white-washed three-rail fence. McGregor decided to stop and consult with the men hidden in the trailer. He would fake a flat, and go about repairing it as he spoke with them.

Albert was happy to leave the claustrophobic stuffiness of the trailer hide and climb the hill with Sykes.

"It looks like an Argentinian stronghold," Sykes said, as they made their way up the embankment. Sykes went on about property and property rights.

"Nelson has worked that land most of his life," Sykes said. "His ancestors did the same." Sweat and tears had dripped into the black soil, and become one with it, Sykes explained. This farm was Kelper land. Any foreigner who illegitimately comes upon it deserves nothing short of death. Their transgression would be redeemed by spilt blood, blood that would nourish the land. Although dirt was just worm droppings, it meant so much more to people. It was the reason they existed. It was how they subsided; the menial tasks it demanded justified their day-to-day existence; a reason to wake in the cold morn, a reason to toil, and a means of feeling closer—one—with the Almighty. Simply: it was worth fighting and dying for.

As they reached the top of the embankment, Albert and Sykes got low and crawled. They crept to a spit of rock and leaned upon it to peer through binoculars. In the figure eight of their vision, they saw men scurry like insects around Nelson's farm. Albert focused on the missiles that

199

threatened the sky. As a pilot, he both feared and respected such advanced weapons.

"Roland II," Albert told Sykes. "Two-stage; Solid propellant; Three-point-five kilogram hollow-charge fragmentation warhead detonated by impact or proximity fuse with a lethal radius of six meters. Cruising speed: Mach one-point-six," he rattled off from training.

Albert and Sykes watched as soldiers came and went from various farm buildings. Albert fixed his view on an officer sitting on the stoop of the farmhouse. He panned his view and spotted several bodies stacked like firewood next to a shed. The bodies were obviously those of civilians, and likely belonged to the family that owned the farm. Albert sighed.

"I count at least 40 soldiers and technicians," Sykes noted. He tapped Albert on the shoulder and pointed to where he should train his binoculars. Albert turned that way and saw the squat sloped hull of an infantry fighting vehicle. It was tracked, had a rear infantry hatch, and a large cannon turret and a missile launcher.

"That's a Marder 1A3," Albert told him. Named for the agile and slender animal native to boreal forests, this German-made machine was a nasty beast with a remote 20 millimeter cannon and Milan missiles. "I have to get this information to friendly forces."

"Your Worshipfulness," Sykes said, using his latest perversion of the proper way to address the Prince, "*we* might be the only friendly forces around." Albert saw the disdain in Sykes's face. Like many islanders, he was angry at the neglect London had shown the Falklands since the last war. Albert knew that Argentina may have been deterred had a larger force been garrisoned here. He also knew that, in a time of huge budget cuts, British forces had been stretched very thin by adventures elsewhere. Down on the road, MacGregor continued the pretense of changing a blown tire. Then, in the corner of his eye, he saw the ground nearby move.

A bush rose up and seemed to grow. Grass suddenly undulated as several shambling mounds of foliage appeared in the field. Instinctively, McGregor reached for the Sterling machine gun perched on the pick-up truck's worn front passenger seat. It was too late, however. He saw the flash and felt the bullets as they ripped into his abdomen. MacGregor's nervous system shut down as one hit his spine. He fell face-first onto the soft seat. MacGregor's last view was of the dashboard's clock. It had dots instead of numbers. His last thought: *That bloody thing hasn't worked in years.*

"Gunfire," Albert said of the echoing crackle. He turned and saw The Warrahs being mowed down. The enemy had popped up from the field. Dressed in yowie suits—camouflaged clothing covered with native foliage—they had sprayed The Warrahs with lethal fire. The soldiers tossed grenades, and fired a rocket-propelled grenade. In short order, the old pick-up and trailer were in flames. Someone—likely Calvert—had forced his way out of the top of the hay-covered hide, but folded over and was engulfed by the flames.

Albert was stunned, his mouth agape. He looked to Sykes who sat crouched beside him. Sykes, too, had a look of surprise, and his eyes widened further as a bullet tore into his forehead. Albert's face was sprayed with brain matter. Sykes's body slumped and Albert moved to catch him.

Disturbingly, he grasped a loose flap of hair-covered skull bone. Albert saw the pink jelly inside the man's skull. With his ears ringing and eyes in tunnel vision, Albert barely heard the helicopter that hopped over the next hill. Yes, his mind screamed run, but Albert's feet were clay.

He managed to stand, however, and the olive-drab aircraft dashed towards him.

The adrenaline waned and Albert's presence of mind returned. He wiped Sykes's blood from his cheek and looked around to decide which way to run. He saw only open fields and the road with the burning truck. Albert sat and lowered his head to his hand. Had he the energy, he might have sobbed.

Albert's head, jaw, and ribs ached bad. He had been punched, knocked unconscious with the butt of a rifle, and kicked in the ribs. Other than the dim light that pushed through a small window, the room was dark. He tried to focus, and spotted a washbasin. *I'm in a cellar*, Albert thought. He saw a table that held a drill, and an array of knives and saws. He turned away, and shifted on the chair in which he sat. His hands and ankles were tightly bound.

A door creaked open and boots came down old wood stairs.

"Prince Albert. I am Major Ezequiel Vargas, 601 Commando Company, *Fuerzas Armadas de la República Argentina*. A pleasure to finally make your acquaintance," Vargas said and went to the table.

"Captain Albert Talbot. His Majesty's Armed Forces. Service number one-two-eight-three-six-four-one-three."

Vargas picked up the electric drill.

"I did not ask you a question," Vargas said with a chuckle.

"Captain Albert--" Albert started to repeat.

"*Silencio.* You have eluded me, embarrassed me, and delivered the wrath of my superiors upon me. For this, you will be punished. I will not kill you—as I am under orders not to—however, I will make you wish that I had."

Albert felt his heart pound in his temples. His breath grew shallow and rapid. *Stay Calm and Carry On*, Albert recited to himself. He decided to go on the offensive against this rather frightening man.

"You are a soldier," Albert said. "You do not fight unfair. To torture a man who is bound and helpless is unfair. It dishonors you. Are you not a man of honor?"

Vargas plugged the electric drill into an outlet.

"This is the horse farm?" Albert asked. "Where is the family that lived here? Dead, I imagine. You are a murderer. You are not a soldier. At least when I killed an innocent, it was an accident."

"You killed--" Vargas started to say, but then stopped himself. His face betrayed internal conflict. Albert pressed further.

"I killed a little girl; flew 9 kilos of high-explosive right into her. Do you have a family, Major Vargas?"

"I had--"

"Did you have a little girl, too?"

Vargas realized he had faltered and he grew angry. He revved the drill, as his defense from guilt or sadness continued to be violence. He moved for Albert and placed the drill bit on the top of his hand. With a high-pitched whine, Vargas started the drill spinning. Albert felt the sharp steel bit tug at his skin. Then it burned and ripped as Vargas drove it through flesh. Albert tried not to scream, but his attempt failed. When he quieted, he heard other soldiers upstairs, laughing as Albert suffered. Vargas's face displayed sadistic satisfaction.

"I will never tell you anything," Albert spat.

"I have not asked you anything," Vargas replied as he steadied the drill on another part of Albert's hand. "We go again, yes?"

"Wanker," Albert bellowed at Vargas.

The drill started up again, and the new hole it made

splattered both men with Albert's blood and tissue.

"I must have hit a vein. *Triste.* Very sorry," Vargas

said with a crooked smile. He waited for Albert to quiet

and calm.

"Hurting me won't bring back your family," Albert

jabbed, though his words were pinched by the raw pain.

"Perhaps you are right. Perhaps I should hurt

another," Vargas said quietly, then yelled: "*Traiga la*

mujer."

Albert did not know Spanish. He did not know that

his tormentor had made an order that would only serve to

ratchet up the torment. Albert heard shuffling upstairs, and

then the cellar door creaked open. Several footfalls

descended the stairs. Albert strained to turn his head and

see what was coming. A soldier had brought a person, a

folded mess of hair and dirty clothes. When that person

looked up, Albert saw it was Linda, bruised and beaten. Vargas's peon pushed her to the floor.

"You know her, don't you?" Vargas asked smugly. Albert would not meet Vargas's or Linda's eyes.

"*Su madre?*" Albert swore; it was a phrase he had heard at a London tapas bar where he had spent joyous evenings of eating and drinking with old mates. Those days seemed so far away. *Perhaps part of another life*, he considered. Vargas went to Linda, stood over her, slid his hand beneath her shirt, and grabbed her left breast. Linda squealed with loathing.

"You do not know her, so you do not mind if I touch her, right?" Vargas said as he fondled Linda's chest.

"Piss off, tosser." Albert's statement was defiant and steadfast, though his heart had broken when he saw Linda and the condition she was in.

"You do know her, then? Well, my men and I now know her *very* well."

"You're a rapist and a murderer. You will burn in hell."

"I will see you there, then, eh, *amigo*?" Vargas's laugh was sickening and exhibited a tenuous grasp on sanity.

"Don't you realize that every time you kill, every time you drill someone's hand, every time you rape, it is your own soul that you are torturing. God will make you pay." Albert saw this last statement worried the Catholic. He would play this line further. "God is always watching— sees all. He will judge you," Albert said with a smile. Vargas fidgeted, so Albert punched again: "You are evil. You are a demon."

"Enough," Vargas bellowed. He turned to Linda, and then grabbed and lifted her chin, forcing her to look to

Albert through swollen eyelids. "I have your friend," Vargas told Linda. "I took your daughter, too." Linda's bloodshot eyes rolled Albert's way. "I raped her before I cut her throat." Linda began to sob. "She squealed with pleasure like a little whore," he twisted the knife of his words. "And, just, before she died, she cried for her mommy, her grandfather, her dog, and her little furry cat."

"*Bastard*," Albert exploded. Although still bound to the chair, he pushed to his feet, and crashed back down as hard as he could. The chair shattered under his body's weight and his strength. Albert stood again. Coils of rope dangled from his wrists and ankles, and bits of wood from the chair fell free. He seemed to grow bigger, inflated by anger, and looked to Vargas. His chest barreled up, and his teeth clenched in an intimidating grimace. The vision made Vargas hesitate. Albert used the moment to throw his full weight and scorn at the smaller man, and he landed an

elbow on Vargas's cheek.

The hit shattered bone and threw Vargas's head back

with a snap, knocking him to the slab floor. Vargas's head

hit hard and started to bleed. Linda stopped crying as

Albert shed the remains of his bindings, went to her, and

lifted her up. She immediately ran to Vargas and kicked his

torso with all her might, breaking her big toe on his ribcage.

Albert pulled her off and she fell into an embrace.

"Kill him," Linda begged.

"No. We are not like him."

"Annie…" Linda had to find her daughter. She had

to find Annie, even if dead. Albert looked at Vargas. He

was curled up on the floor, and his head had a big knot that

protruded from his crew cut. He bled from his mouth, too,

and his bit tongue hung from between red-stained teeth.

Albert spotted an assault rifle propped up in a corner of the basement.

"Jackpot."

It was Vargas's personal rifle. Albert picked up the cold weapon, released the magazine to check its load, smacked it in again, and cycled the charging handle. "Nice." It was an FN FAL 50.61 with a folding-stock and shortened barrel. "Fabrique Nationale de Herstal Fusil Automatique Léger."

"Eh?" Linda was perplexed.

"A Belgian light automatic rifle. Paratrooper version." Albert folded the stock and brought the weapon to his hip. "Stay quiet and stay close."

Linda grabbed some of Albert's shirt and shadowed him as he moved up the stairs. He hunched down, the weapon's sight floating before his eye. All British Army Air Corps pilots are infantrymen first, and Albert's own

Infantry Training Centre skills rushed back. He could almost hear his trainer screaming in his ear. Hundreds of years of warrior tradition flowed through him, from his heart, through his brain, to his legs and to his trigger finger. With Linda in trail, Albert bounded up the stairs and through the cellar door.

The sudden look of surprise on the Argentine soldiers face forestalled any decisive action. As he sipped a cup of coffee in the house's kitchen, he never expected anyone other than Vargas to emerge from the basement. The look on the soldier's expression was priceless to Albert; almost comical. That look was locked in by death when Albert put a single 7.62 x 51 millimeter NATO round between mister coffee drinker's eyes. Albert spun around. He clicked his weapon to full automatic, and hosed the men standing at the farmhouse's kitchen counter. They had made sandwiches from the cold cuts in the refrigerator, and, now, slumped and fell against the cabinets. Smeared blood marked the trail of their dead fall. They all had the same look of surprise, a sickening realization that their days of glory had ended. Albert and Linda heard the whimper of a child. They looked to each other and grinned.

"Annie," Linda exclaimed.

"It came from in there," Albert said as he gestured toward a door. He went to it and kicked it in.

Annie was tied to a bed. Linda rushed in, untied the ropes, and scooped her up. Immediately, she covered Annie's dirty face with kisses and squeezed her tight.

Argentine soldiers reacted to the ruckus downstairs, their boots stomping along the farmhouse's second floor hall. Linda looked to Albert; the look uniquely female: It asked: 'Will you protect me and my little girl?' Albert wondered if the mother of the child at Jugroom Fort had had that same look. If she had looked that way as the men that had driven the SUV honked the horn outside her hut; and, had likely assured her that her little girl would be just fine, but then she spotted that missile that flew its way in to kill her family. .

"Don't worry," Albert assured Linda. He picked up one of the dead soldier's pistols and handed it to her butt first. "Can you use one of these?"

Linda press-checked the chamber, found it empty, and cycled the slide to load a round.

Albert looked out the kitchen windows and then opened the farmhouse's back door just a crack.

"Alright then," he said. "It looks clear. Move out. I'll cover you."

Albert knelt; his weapon aimed down the hallway and directly at the sounds that rushed at them. Linda immediately complied and tugged at Annie.

"Mommy," Annie mumbled, jerking this way and that. The tone of the little girl's voice made it clear how distraught she had become, and that she longed for the familiarity and safety of home.

Albert saw a face that peeked around a corner, and then an arm emerged, holding a gun that fired with a deafening flash. The rounds ripped into the wood-paneled wall next to him. Then Albert heard whispers in Spanish as Argentine soldiers stacked up and prepared to charge down the hall. Somebody chucked a grenade that landed with a metallic clunk, and rolled at him. Albert jumped out the open back door where he found Linda and Annie sitting in a car with the motor running. The grenade exploded in the kitchen, blowing out the window glass.

"Get in," Linda shouted. Albert piled in and readied his rifle to cover their retreat. "Keys were in it," Linda said with a nervous laugh as she peeled out.

"Get down and stay down," Albert told Annie who was in the back seat. Linda spun the tires and revved the engine into its tachometer gauge's red zone. The car skidded along the muddy road that led from the farmhouse. Extending the FAL rifle's folding stock, Albert trained the weapon on the farmhouse's back door, and fired when two soldiers rushed out. Annie cried, covering her ears. The Argentines ran smack into Albert's bullets and fell back against the house.

"Bastards," Albert yelled at the dead men and he then bounced into the car's roof. Annie giggled when he came back down and at his funny grimace. The white farmhouse grew smaller in the car's rear window. Albert realized his adopted weapon was now empty. He tossed it to the floor by his feet.

Vargas went to the upstairs bedroom. His sniper had his rifle poked outside, tracking the fleeing car.

"*Yo tengo una oportunidad, mayor*," the man reported that he had a shot.

"*¿De quién?*" 'On who?' Vargas asked.

"*El conductor. La mujer.*" The driver—the woman—was in his sights.

"*Alto el fuego*," a frustrated Vargas told his sniper to hold fire.

"*¿Mayor?*" the man questioned the order.

"*Le dije*: *Alto el fuego*," Vargas repeated the order. He turned to leave and give chase once again. He stopped in the doorframe and turned back to the kneeling sniper. "*Si usted recibe un disparo en el príncipe, llévelo*," Vargas told the man to shoot if he got a clear shot on the Prince.

"*Si, mayor.*"

◊◊◊◊

The adrenalin waned and Albert became aware of the throb in his hand. He looked at it. The two punctures were caked with dry blood, and his palm was hamburger. He opened the glove compartment and found a paisley scarf that he wrapped around the wound.

The dirt road pushed the car around. Deep tractor ruts channeled its small wheels, and its nearly bare tire treads barely gripped the slop. They reached the apex of a small hill. Linda slammed on the brakes. They locked up, and the car slid along a bit further before it stopped. Ahead sat an armored vehicle, its cannon and missile launcher pointed their way.

"Out of the car, now," Albert shouted.

8: TANGO

"Hell is yourself and the only redemption is when a person puts himself aside to feel deeply for another person."—Tennessee Williams

Albert did not wait for Linda to react to his order to vacate the car. He reached back and lifted Annie into his lap, tucked her in tight, and tugged Linda along as he rolled out and onto the grass. As they all hit the ground, it began to rain. They rolled behind a rock, and Albert pushed Annie and Linda down. Then he stole a peek at the Argentine Marder infantry fighting vehicle.

The Marder's cannon muzzle flashed. Sparks flew as the big rounds ripped into their little escape car. The car jumped and shook as it was torn apart, and then it burst into flames when the gas tank was hit and ignited. Albert felt the resultant heat dry his eyeballs. Annie cried and Linda screamed. Albert pulled them both on top of him and began to roll down a small embankment. They landed in a streambed.

The icy cold water stole their breath. Rain pelted them hard. Albert sat up. The rain became a downpour, falling in sheets.

"Not our day, is it?" Albert said to Linda, a crooked smile on his face. Linda forced herself to smile back. Even soaked, exhausted, and bruised, Linda was a beauty, Albert once again realized. He leaned in and kissed her. Then he offered a jealous Annie a compensatory peck on the cheek. "Come on," he said with urgent big eyes. Albert tugged them along the stream, and started to circle to the side of the threat. They heard and felt the rumble of the armored vehicle's big engine.

The Marder rumbled along the road. Its tracks spat rocks and mud, and the infantry fighting vehicle was soon alongside the stream, high above where Albert, Annie, and Linda snuggled up to an eroded bank. Pebbles and clumps of dirt fell upon them, and they felt the reverb of the engine in their chest, smelled the sooty diesel, and crossed their fingers, hoping it would pass them by. After a moment, they agreed that they had not been seen.

When certain that the vehicle had moved on, they clawed and slipped their way up the embankment, and peeked over the precipice through the tall grass. Their car was still ablaze, but now a truck approached. It stopped short of the wreck. Linda gasped and Annie cringed as Vargas and several soldiers dismounted. The infantry fighting vehicle had stopped several hundred yards beyond. Albert saw terror in the eyes of Annie and Linda.

"Annie seems okay. Scared, but okay" Albert whispered to Linda. He smiled at Annie as she grasped a fist-full of mud and grass. Albert's face turned solemn. He gently brushed a finger across Linda's warm, rosy cheek, and ventured, "Did that bastard really…touch you?"

"Just what you saw. Just my left knocker, there in the cellar," Linda said with a crooked half-smile. She saw the seriousness in Albert's stare, and summarized "No. He did not. His men tried, but he stopped them." Albert looked again at Vargas, who scurried about the road, ducking between licks of fire and smoke, and giving orders. Albert wondered about the man. He saw him in the distortion of heat, and looked to be the demon Albert had accused him of being. Then Albert realized this was too simplistic, and wondered about his enemy's true nature. *He is just a man*, Albert concluded. *Just a flawed man…like me.*

Vargas shielded his face from the heat and inspected the interior of the charred car his prisoners had escaped in. He saw only burning seats; no bodies. Vargas straightened up and scanned the terrain. Pointing, he ordered soldiers off in different directions. The Marder's turret began to scan the area as its imagery system was brought to bear.

Vargas's boots clanged on a cow grate that spanned the road. He ran his fingers through tall grass waving above the drainage ditch that marked the road's edge. He could sense his quarry. Certain they were close by, he felt drawn to their presence. Vargas closed his eyes. His mind's eye was like a drone, flying over the undulating earth, scanning the folds and troughs of terrain, and zeroing in on where the man, woman, and child hid. Vargas looked at the glass lenses of the Marder's turret imaging system. He knew this lifeless bug-eyed bank of lenses would not be the way to find those that had escaped him.

Vargas's greatest motivation was not a hatred for the British Prince, not lust for the woman, nor jealousy of the innocent ignorance still prevalent in a pre-adolescent girl, it was that Doctor Amsel would not accept any excuses. Vargas's own reputation and standing stood starkly in jeopardy. He knew that if he did not capture Prince Albert and bring him back to be used as leverage, he too might find himself in the basements of the old building at Avenida 25 de Mayo. Vargas would rather kill the Prince than fail. He would rather die himself than fail. However, as he had learned unexpectedly, he would not harm the woman or little girl.

The ghosts of his own family had taught him this, as he stood over the bound child, his sharp V-42 combat knife in hand. Those animals had wanted to rape and hurt the ladies. Vargas, however, confirmed something he had suspected before: He had something in common with his

British enemy, and had a semblance of chivalry. Although he had killed men before—men he saw as soldiers in a war against his homeland and regime—Vargas realized he, too, was truly a soldier. Tired of such musings, Vargas drew his Star pistol and strolled off. Soldiers asked after him, and, like the dogs they were, Vargas told them to stay.

When the moment presented itself, and before the enemy spotted them again, Albert, Annie, and Linda ran for the next hill, slipping and sliding. The rain was both a hindrance and a blessing. It limited visibility, weighed down the grass, and concealed their passage. They topped the hill and glided down the opposite side. Albert stopped them when he saw a small, olive-drab disk sticking out of the mud.

"What?" Linda asked as she looked about frantically. She tugged Albert's shirt; her husband's old one. "Let's go," she insisted, ignorant of the potential instant death which surrounded her.

Albert held Annie still. He raised his bloody hand up and signaled Linda not to move. She recognized the earnestness of his facial expression and froze obediently. Albert studied the ground. He saw more of the disks poking up from the ground. And then it hit him, others were arrayed behind them, between them, and where they had just been. Albert gasped when he realized another was right next to Linda's foot.

"Don't move an inch."

"What are they?"

"Mines. Anti-personnel mines," Albert said, knowing that, for every one he saw, there were likely several more buried types, and others still that were capable of stopping a tank. He wiped his sweaty face and leaned down to study one device, and recognized the pressure fuse as belonging to a Brazilian-made T-AB-1 land-mine.

"Mines?" Linda said and began to shake visibly. "Annie, stay where you are," she told her daughter. He voice was as shaky as her body.

"See that disk by your foot?" Albert asked. "Whatever you do, keep off it...off of them." Albert pointed to the other plastic shapes surrounding them. He realized the farmhouse represented an area command headquarters of sorts, and that the Argentines had sown the approaches with defensive fields. Turning, he could see their last steps, muddy footprints that had filled with rain water. Annie seemed to be beyond the edge of the field. Albert was thankful her little legs had made her slower.

"Okay. Step exactly where I do," Albert told Linda. He moved slowly and carefully, and lowered his boot into the depression of his last step's print. He realized Linda's eyes were rolling back in their sockets;   She was about to faint. She wavered and Albert struggled to support her weight. His mangled hand failed, and Linda almost dragged him down as she collapsed into the mud. Annie shrieked, and Albert waited for the explosion that would kill them all. If Linda's weight triggered an anti-personnel mine, it would jump up out of the ground, explode a few feet up, and spray them with deadly shrapnel and ball bearings. If it were an anti-tank mine, she was likely too light to trigger it. However, if she did, there would be a massive explosion. They would all disappear, leaving just a pink mist floating over a crater. As long moments passed, nothing happened.

"Fancy that," Albert said with a stressed giggle. For now, he thought, Linda was better off unconscious. He scooped Linda up and folded her over his shoulder. Albert sank into the mud and struggled to escape its suction. He squinted to see in the downpour, and, as gracefully as he could, egressed from the periphery of the minefield, and toward little, bawling Annie. When they were back on the slope, and he was certain they were clear of any signs of the minefield, Albert flopped Linda into the grass. With aching legs, he plopped down. Annie went to Linda and shook her. She was unable to rouse her mother.

"Your mum is all right, Anne. Don't worry." Albert rolled onto his belly, scurried up the hillside, and peeked over the crest. The rainfall continued to be heavy, and a mist had risen from the ground. He could hear the Argentine armored vehicle off in the distance, and the voices of a search party. A bell began to toll.

A church spire poked from the fog that blanketed the island. The bell rang out 12 times. Its din—despite the rain and intermittent rumbles of thunder—carried and echoed. Albert scanned east and saw a barn.

The barn's roof shingles shone green with moss. Its brown wood wallboards were worn and weathered. Fronds of hay poked from between these boards, and little round holes showed where knots had fallen out of the wood. Albert decided this structure would be their immediate objective, a place to hole up, rest, and defend until nightfall. Linda moaned.

"Linda, come on, wake up now," he said, gently patting her face.

"Mum. Mummy, time to get up," Annie added.

Linda's eyes opened and briefly rolled in their sockets. Albert lifted her head by the chin. She looked at him, and then to her daughter. Both girls smiled widely. Annie dropped onto Linda and mugged her with hugs and kisses. Then Annie peeled off her mother to hug Albert. She squeezed him as hard as her little arms could manage.

"I love you," Annie declared to Albert. Those three words warmed him to the depths of his soul. They went in and uncovered the guilt, lifted it, and took it from his shoulders. Albert felt lighter, and he felt a nagging worry that he supposed fathers must feel: that he had to do everything in his power to protect this little sprite, to keep her safe, and to shield her from evil and death, with his very own being if need be.

"There's a barn a few hills over," Albert told Linda. "That where we're going. So, I need you to stand up and walk. Understood?"

Linda focused, nodded, and stumbled to her feet. She leaned on her helpful daughter to steady her steps. Albert leading the way, they stayed low, skirted small valleys, and used tall grass and large rocks to cover their movement. The rain began to let up. Sunshine broke through and burned away the mist. The grey that had covered the landscape yielded, and a rainbow burst forth, shooting from the ground and into the sky. Flowers that had been muted in the deluge seemed to light up as though suddenly plugged in. Their colors sang again, and they swayed in the breeze. Albert took a deep breath, and, for the first time, realized the truth of beauty of the land he was traversing. He looked back on the last few days, and realized that, as terrifying as they were, they also satisfied.

He could feel the buzz; probably more lack of sleep than pride at having stayed alive for this long. Albert suddenly understood the high of the infantryman. Although he had felt the wonder of the fight from the sky, he could now relate with the man that fought in the dirt, and looked another man in the eyes before plunging a bayonet between his ribs. Albert wondered that if man felt joy from such a dark experience, perhaps his nature truly was evil. Then he realized that, by weaving moments of good among those that were evil, man could tip his nature to goodness, could rise above, could shun the Devil and let God in. *It's about choice*, he thought. *We are plunged into situations that reveal our true selves. We are living a test, and there will be a reckoning when it is all over; a counting of the coin, pluses and minuses, a spreadsheet of life*

Albert suddenly knew that all were being judged, that there was a panel taking score, whether the Pagan plethora of observers, or the one true reckoner, our chits were being counted. Although he knew he had killed—snuffed the innocent—it would be understood, he believed, that it had been a dreadful mistake. He had mourned even before the missile's impact. Also, he had, after all, tried to stop it. Albert looked to Annie who stuck out her finger so that a butterfly fluttering about might land there. With the warming sun on his face, Albert watched the delicate insect alight on Annie, concluded that the human spirit was beautiful and it survived by nurturing itself on simple things. Albert pulled Linda in close and walked for a moment with his arm about her. Annie snuggled up too, and the three of them walked together among the wild flowers and tall grass. The little barn was their immediate goal, and Albert thought it best not to look too far ahead, to think too much. It was far better to feel what was immediate, to live the moment, and thank the universe for giving you breath enough to say: "I love you both." Linda looked deep into Albert, saw his pain and feelings, and smiled. She felt at home in the deep brown pools of his sad eyes.

Trying to make the best of the lack of cover, Albert, Annie, and Linda moved toward the barn. When they reached it without being seen, they crouched at one of its walls. Albert slid the door open and checked inside.

"It's a hay loft. We should be able to get some rest."

He spotted a bin full of potatoes and a small, dripping spigot. "And perhaps something to eat and drink."

As soon as they entered, Annie collapsed onto a bed of straw and fell asleep. Albert started to check the potatoes. While a few felt too mushy, several others were edible. He handed one to Linda and took a drink from the tap. Gulping mouthfuls, Albert realized how dehydrated he was. Linda took her turn after chewing some raw spud. She, too, drank deep. With her belly full, Linda lay down beside Annie. Exhausted, Albert collapsed his weight to the floor like an imploded building.

"I'll keep first watch," he mumbled.

"Want this?" Linda offered the pistol. He waved it away. Linda took a deep breath, maybe two, and fell fast asleep.

Even though he tried his best to stay awake, Albert also succumbed to exhaustion, and, with head rested on bent knees, was soon snoring.

◇◇◇◇

Vargas put his hand to Annie's mouth. She awakened and tried to scream. Vargas collected her in his arms. Linda felt the disturbance beside her. She opened an eye. About to scream, too, she decided against it when she saw the Argentinian. He had a gold-sparkled grin, and he had Annie, a big knife to her soft, pink neck.

"*Eduardo Talbot*," Vargas said loudly, the disdain he had for the name was evident. Albert snapped awake and sprang to his feet. About to lunge at Vargas, he stopped himself. His body twitched as his brain countermanded the command sent to his muscles. His tired mind was unable to conjure anything creative. It was time to surrender. Albert looked to Linda. Her worried eyes bulged, and her teeth ground with hatred and with helplessness.

"Annie will be fine, Linda," Albert consoled. "I promise." Albert turned to Annie, and said: "Annie, baby, you will be fine. Okay?" Annie whimpered and clenched her eyes shut. This squeezed out a tear that rolled slowly down her blushed cheek. Albert turned his attention to Vargas.

Flames replaced sadness in Albert's eyes. They flickered and licked at the squinted lids. He just wanted to kill. He would take true satisfaction in twisting Vargas's neck until it snapped.

"How's the hand, *caballero*?" Vargas taunted.

Albert lifted his wrapped hand to show him, painfully extending the middle finger, and smiled wide.

"Still works," Albert snickered. "Let her go. *Now*."

Vargas fumed and pressed the cold blade to Annie's throat. Annie went wooden.

"If you harm her--" Albert warned.

"What? What will you do?"

Albert thought to say, 'I will kill you,' but he decided on another way.

"You are a worm," Albert said. "You hide behind a uniform and a flag, but you are just a worm."

"No," Vargas said defensively but also visibly rattled. Then he took a deep breath and calmed himself. "I am a fisherman, and *this* is my worm." Vargas pressed the knife against Annie a bit harder. "Now, get on my hook, Prince Albert."

"Albert, please. Do as he says," Linda begged. Albert saw little choice but to comply. Vargas recognized this realization in the way Albert's puffed chest fell.

"Get on your knees, and put your hands behind your head."

Albert complied.

"Now, cross your legs," Vargas ordered.

Albert did it.

With the Prince now a diminished threat, Vargas grabbed a handful of Annie's hair, put the knife away, and took out his pistol.

When Linda saw the gun, she remembered the one she had tucked into her hay bed. She remembered she had chambered a round back at the farmhouse. *The safety is on,* she thought. *I will have to be quick.* As if reading her mind, Vargas turned his attention Linda's way.

"You. Do the same: hands on head, get on your knees, and cross your legs." Linda knelt as close to where the gun was stashed as possible. Vargas tugged at Annie's hair to get her to kneel, too. Annie yelped and began to cry hard. Vargas moved his pistol's point of aim from Albert to Linda and back again. Vargas let go of Annie and pawed for his radio with his freed hand. He found it and clicked the transmit button.

"*Culebra zero-dos-uno*," he spoke into the radio. When feedback chirped, he used his gun hand to adjust the squelch dial on the little walkie-talkie.

Linda's heart pounded. Her throat was dry. She dove for the hay and felt the butt of the gun. Vargas realized she was in motion and began to unfold his arm as he hurried to line up the gun barrel on Linda again. During this moment, Linda was able to raise her weapon, disengage the safety, and get a sight picture. With the dot of her pistol's front sight settled on Vargas's chest, Linda squeezed the trigger. Just like her father had taught her, Linda made sure not to jerk the gun as she fired. The gun yapped.

Vargas was shoved onto his back. He dropped the radio, and, though he held onto his pistol, it was now pointed at the ceiling. Linda rushed over and stood over him. Vargas's radio pleaded for a response.

Still conscious, Vargas struggled to breathe, and tried to talk. Only blood bubbles and a gurgle came forth. If he could have been understood, Albert, Annie, and Linda would have heard Vargas say his dead wife's name. Vargas smiled and began to sweep his gun toward Albert who had begun to get up. Linda's final shot was to Vargas's head. It burst like a ruptured cantaloupe and sprayed the hay with red wetness. Linda dropped the smoking gun and dove for Annie. She wrapped her in her arms and whispered words of love in her ears. Annie tried to look at Vargas, but Linda covered her eyes and spoke more whispers of reassurance.

"Is he dead?" Annie asked with the morbid curiosity of the young.

"He will not bother us again," Linda offered instead of confirmation. Albert went to them both and joined the hug. All three looked up when they heard an engine.

"What now?" Albert asked. He went to the wall to peek out. There, framed by the weathered boards, was the Argentine infantry fighting vehicle and several soldiers. They had crested the hill and now headed toward the little barn. Albert turned back to Linda. From his anguished look, she could tell it was bad news. Linda exhaled hard. Soon, voices, mingled with the ever-increasing mechanical rumble.

"More company," he said with a sigh. "And that won't be of any help," Albert said as he pointed at the pistol on the hay pile. He went to it and picked it up anyway, engaged the safety, and tucked it in his pocket. He returned to his vigil at the wall, and watched the approach of the enemy vehicle. Their little barn stuck out like a sore thumb.

It was an obvious point of interest, a place on everyone's list, it would seem. "Bollocks," he mumbled.

Albert slid down the wall and onto his bottom. Annie and Linda simply stared at him. Their eyes begged Albert to think of a plan of action. He had none to offer. Annie and Linda jumped when they heard the explosion, and then Annie cried at the gunfire that followed. Albert and Linda held their breath, eyes wide as they awaited the impact of fire, as they waited for rounds to rip through the walls, and to tear into them all. Annie just cried louder and began to hyperventilate. She would pass out soon, Albert thought. *Probably better for her.* Albert and Linda looked to one another when they heard a shout that could only be English. Albert jumped up and peeked out again.

The Argentine infantry fighting vehicle was burning. A fountain of fire erupted from the vehicle's upper hatch, and a jagged hole in its side belched smoke. Dead bodies lay scattered about, each grotesquely posed. Forms

emerged from the grass. If not for their movement, their

camouflage made them all but invisible. Albert saw one of

the soldiers lowering a thick pipe from his shoulder. He

recognized it as the launch tube for a British NLAW anti-

tank weapon.

"Could it be?" Albert wondered aloud.

"What is it?" Linda asked, excited by the look on

Albert's face.

"I think--" He looked out again. "I think we're

saved." Albert recognized Major Fagan. "It's Fagan. It's

the SAS." Albert slid the barn door open, stepped out, and

waved.

Seeing a man in civilian clothing, the SAS troop ran

toward him with their rifles at the ready. When Major

Fagan recognized Albert, his relief was evident. He

signaled his men to fan out and encircle the barn. Then, with a big smile, Fagan approached Prince Albert.

"Captain Talbot," Fagan said as he stomped one foot after the other, and snapped a crisp salute. "Thank goodness you are all right."

Albert, Annie, and Linda ate everything the commandos could put out. There was peanut butter, jelly, and crackers; franks and beans; and an orange drink full of electrolytes and vitamins. One of the men—a Lieutenant Hayden—folded the food wrappers and made intricate animal shapes. He gave them to Annie. She placed them in the grass and played. Major Fagan told Albert it was time to move.

As they all marched single file across the land, Fagan explained that via a captured Argie radio, they had learned of Albert's presence in the barn. They passed the burning

Marder. Albert buried Annie's face in his chest so she would not see the dead soldiers.

One of the SAS—a Welshman—began to hum a tune. Soon, the entire SAS troop sang softly as they weaved their way along a cow path:

"May this fair land we love so well/ In Dignity and freedom dwell/ While worlds may change and go awry/ Whilst there is still one voice to cry/ There'll always be an England/ While there's a country lane/ Wherever there's a cottage small; Beside a field of grain/ There'll always be an England."

They all came over a hill and looked down upon the horse farm. The Argentine surface-to-air missile battery had been blown, and its wreckage continued to smolder in the field. From the hilltop, a trench-line was visible.

The trench had been dug around the farmhouse, and had small sandbag-lined redoubts; ceiling-less rooms excavated from the countryside. Behind the wider main line stretched a smaller, shoulder-width travel trench. It made Albert think of World War I, but also of one-dimensional thinking. If Albert were in an Apache and saw such earthworks, he would spray the area with his rockets to remind the defenders that there were three dimensions to space, one of which was air. However, Albert now moved on the ground, in infantry territory. He suddenly understood the doctrinaire types that had ordered the trenches dug. He saw that part of the trench-line had been filled-in, used to bury those killed when, in close quarter combat, using handguns and grenades, and under the protection of their sniper, the SAS had swept the trench line. Albert could see one neat mound of dirt in the grass. He looked questioningly to Fagan.

"His name was Ravensdale. He jumped on an Argie grenade; saved his mates. I'm putting him in for a Meritorious Service Medal."

"I'm sorry," Albert offered. Fagan nodded thanks and walked off to hide the emotion that came with losing a close friend on the field of battle.

Fagan signaled his men to form a perimeter, and then sent a few of them to check the farmhouse and stables again.

Completing this sweep, they commandeered an Argentine troop truck and jeep from the farmhouse garage, and transferred petrol from a tractor.

Albert, Annie, and Linda rode in the jeep with Major Fagan and two others, while the rest of the SAS troop followed closely in the truck. Annie succumbed to the smooth road and vibration of the engine, and fell deep asleep in Linda's lap.

"Where are we headed?" Albert inquired of Fagan.

"Button Bay."

A black phantom, the American nuclear attack submarine United States Ship *California* hovered off the shallows of the Falkland's Choiseul Sound, just east of Lively Island. USS *California,* of the vaunted *Virginia*-class, had recently come out of repair and refit at Electric Boat in Groton, Connecticut. Exercising in the deeps of the Puerto Rico Trench, she had been ordered to race to the South Atlantic. Captained by Commander Max Wolff, *California* had made a speed course for latitude -52°, longitude -55°, and arrived on station within days.

California had then poked her stealthy electronic surveillance and photonics masts above the rolling surface, and sucked in new orders from an orbiting satellite. Wolff was handed the printout and a cup of coffee. He read them with little reaction, though when he passed them to his executive officer, the man's brow furled, and he uttered a single word: "Interesting." Wolff then ordered a stealthy approach to the islands some 120 miles to the west.

Among *California*'s load-out of Mark-48 torpedoes and Tomahawk cruise missiles, the boat sported another deadly weapon: US Navy SEALs. SEAL stood for Sea, Air, Land Teams. Each team comprised a 13-man platoon, and *California* had aboard Team 5 out of Coronado, California. The SEALs had been briefed, and now prepared for the coming action in the submarine's staging berth.

A burly, balding lieutenant was the officer-in-charge. Known as 'Bullfrog' to his fellow SEALs, he had eaten lots of dirt, sand, and water on many missions, including with Task Force K-Bar which cleared the cave complex of Afghanistan's Zhawar Kili; the team that surveyed the Iraqi oil terminals of Al-Basra and Khawr al-Amaya; and, as a participant of the Al-Faw campaign.

The SEALs donned black rubber wetsuits that made them appear their namesake, and they gathered their dive equipment and weapons. A petty officer entered the staging berth. He informed the operators that the submarine was in position and had clear scopes. Grunts of acknowledgment met this news, as the men continued about their routine.

One operator inserted a magazine into his .45 caliber Universal Self-loading Pistol, press-checked for an empty chamber, and holstered the firearm. Bullfrog mounted a tactical light to the Picatinny rail of his Mark-17 Special Forces combat assault rifle. Although some SEALs carried the Mark-16 which fired the standard 5.56-millimeter NATO, he preferred the -17, chambered with the larger 7.62-millimeter round. Bullfrog finished his preparations by attaching a large ammunition drum to his rifle, wiggled it to assure proper seating, and then grabbed for his 9-millimeter sidearm. Slapping a magazine into the handgun, he racked the slide and manipulated the decocker, lowering the hammer for safe carry on a chambered round. Bullfrog then turned his attention to the rest of his teammates.

The assistant officer-in-charge loaded his own weapons and the platoon chief was busy distributing grenades to the others. The platoon's leading petty officer delivered a brief speech to the SEALs, reiterating their roles in the mission, as well as the ever-present price of failure. Then, one by one, the SEALs looked to their leader. Bullfrog stood, occupying much of the space in the cramped compartment.

"Okay, we are all jocked up," he said. "There are 1,600 fathoms beneath the keel. We've got a two-mile round trip using scooters from the sail. Wally, that's you," he pointed at one of his team and got a nod in return. "Ops team is using re-breathers. Okay, ready to get wet and sandy?"

"Hooyah," was the answer that echoed in the berth. Nine SEALs entered the lockout trunk located just aft of *California's* sail. Once inside, Bullfrog clanged the hatch shut and spun its wheel tight, as the SEALs got out their Dräger re-breathers—small self-contained breathing units that filter exhaled air and supplement it with fresh, all without releasing telltale bubbles. With everyone's fins, tanks, and re-breathers in place, Bullfrog got a thumbs-up from the men.

Bullfrog actuated a lever that jutted from among pipes on the trunk's wall. There was a trickle from a screen mesh-covered outlet, and then a rush of icy seawater as the chamber began to flood. Clumps of foam spun as the water rose quickly in the confines. Once the trunk was full and equalized—matching the pressure outside *California's* hull—Bullfrog looked for a second round of thumbs-up from his SEALs. With everyone's equipment working properly, he got the confirmation he needed. He unlocked the outer hatch. The SEALs swam up and out of the trunk, and into the blackness of the Atlantic Ocean.

Emerging from the submarine's steel casing, the SEALs gathered by the hatch, a pod of warrior animals hovering in the deep. *California* was rock steady as she hovered beneath the undulating silver surface. Fighting a current, the SEALs followed glowing green lights toward the boat's sail. The first swimmer shone his light there, while another SEAL swam over to the storage lockers dotting its vertical side.

One locker was opened. Several bullet-shaped black scooters were removed and distributed to the team. Although each man was a world-class athlete, the vehicles would cut down on transit time and unnecessary fatigue.

Another locker sprang open. A SEAL pulled out two plastic cylinders that contained collapsed inflatable boats. Four more SEALs exited the lockout trunk on *California*'s spine and swam to assemble with the rest of their team. With the trunk's outer hatch shut, Bullfrog took a compass reading, and pointed into the distance. They started their scooters, moved along the submarine's hull, and then passed over *California*'s extended dive planes and domed bow. Headed for the outer beach of East Falkland Island's Button Bay, the 13 combat swimmers were quickly swallowed by dark waters. With her special forces away, *California* nosed down and went deep.

A thick soup of shore fog veiled the rocky sand of Button Bay's beach, and gentle waves rhythmically lapped it. There was a glint off a diver's mask. Gaping barrels and silhouettes emerged from the surf. The SEALs slowly and silently came ashore and disappeared into the swaying brush that lined the beach's crest.

Up the embankment, just beyond the line of seaweed that marked high-tide, among clumps of tall grass, the members of SEAL Team 5 waited. They were plants and rocks to anyone who might have been watching. They allowed Fagan and his SAS troop to walk up on them before standing. Bullfrog looked to the woman and child accompanying the Prince and the SAS troop.

"Who the hell are these people?" Bullfrog demanded, his eyes and teeth standing out bright against the black grease paint on his face. "I have orders to retrieve one royal pain in the ass, no one else," he said, with the apparent contempt of a colonial.

Albert turned to Fagan, and said: "Major, I am not leaving this island without them."

"Captain, I will get them to safety, get them to Mount Pleasant air base."

"Negative. They are coming with me. That's an order." His eyes bored into Bulldog.

Annie and Linda looked to Albert and smiled. Major Fagan went to the American. They huddled for a talk.

Annie shuffled over to the other Americans. These were the first she had ever met, and could not resist asking where they were from.

"New York," one SEAL said.

"Oh, I have seen it in movies," Annie grew excited. "And you, mister?"

"California."

"Oh. Ever been to Disneyland?" she asked with a bounce. The SEAL smiled and nodded yes. Annie pointed to the next man.

"Elkhart, Indiana."

"Never heard of it," Annie declared, and the SEAL chuckled. She continued, "Mister?"

"Florida."

"Florida. Sounds nice and warm." Annie turned to the next shadow that knelt in the grass with his rifle pointed at the dirt.

"Texas, little missy. Austin, Texas."

"Ever been to the Alamo?" Annie asked, having read all about the famous fort in school.

"All right," Bullfrog interrupted, "That's enough chit-chat. Let's get out of here."

Annie mumbled, "Sorry," and retreated to her mother's arm. She whispered that the Americans spoke English in a funny way.

A few moments later, Albert, Annie, and Linda were aboard inflatable boats and motored with the SEALs out onto Choiseul Sound. The SAS took up position on the beach to cover their escape. Albert waved to Fagan. Fagan waved back. SEALs were prone in the bows, searching for Argentine patrol boats.

The inflatables sped past Middle Island, and out to the Argentine Sea, and as the ride grew rougher and the Falklands sank on the horizon line, a shape appeared ahead. It was long and black, and its back was covered with drops of water that sparkled in the moonlight.

"Look, mummy, there's some sort of sea monster," Annie said. Linda squinted to see the form that loomed larger and larger as they approached. Soon they were alongside the long, cylindrical hull of *California*. Commander Wolff stood there, as did the executive officer and other officers-of-the-watch. Despite the danger, they had surfaced the submarine for the rendezvous. The SEALs and their guests were hustled aboard. As soon as they were inside and the hatches closed, Commander Wolff returned his boat to her natural element: deep beneath the waves.

As Albert, Annie, and Linda climbed down ladders and stairs, *California*'s hull popped and groaned with submergence. Invited to share the captain's quarters, they showered and got tucked into the bed and spare bunks. All three fell fast asleep.

In the morning, *California* met a launch from South Georgia Island's British Antarctic Survey Research Station at King Edward Point. Albert, Annie, and Linda were brought ashore where they boarded a C-130 Hercules that skied its way from an ice field and into the air. From on high, Albert admired the rippled cobalt-blue ice of the glaciers. *The land is bejeweled*, he thought.

The Hercules met an air force KC3 Voyager tanker over the Atlantic Ocean. It maneuvered its refueling probe into a drogue that trailed behind the big twin-engine jet and topped off the Herky Bird's tanks. Several hours later the Hercules landed on the long runway of RAF Ascension Island.

Silhouetted by the sunset, Albert, Annie, and Linda boarded a BAe 146 regional airliner for the final leg back to England.

"Son," King Edward bellowed as Albert walked into Balmoral's Drawing Room. The blue walls, gold trim, and plaid carpet momentarily mesmerized the Prince. Back in uniform, and hand healing satisfactorily, Albert longed for the soft shirt and pants Linda had gifted him. He shifted where he stood, itchy from the wool that draped his now thinner body, and again uncomfortable from the color and opulence of the room.

"Your Majesty," Albert said with a formal dip of the head.

"Father. Father…Or, Dad, for goodness sake." For the first time in ages, King Edward embraced his son. "Welcome home," he whispered into Albert's ear. Albert froze, unsure of how to respond, and then patted his father on the back. "Well, then," the King pushed Albert back. He held him by the shoulders and shook him gently. "We owe those Americans thanks for getting you home safe." Albert smiled, having learned that no British submarine had been near enough, and, that the American president—an admitted Anglophile—had insisted on lending a hand. "Well, let us celebrate your safe return. Come. We will have some lunch and tea," he said, and then muttered under his breath: "And perhaps a warming drink or two." Albert felt a bit frightened by his father's joviality and familiarity, all of which felt forcefully exuberant. King Edward put his arm around Albert as they left the Drawing Room for the Gallery. Light streamed through the tall windows. The grey stone of the Gallery seemed warmer than Albert remembered, but the patterned carpet, as hypnotic as ever. King Edward and Prince Albert turned into the Corridor, then through the tall, intricately carved double doors that led to the Dining Room.

It has its own sky, Albert thought of the Dining Room's vaulted ceiling. Although he had eaten and played in the room many times before, the paneled, portrait-laden walls had never stared at him so, the heights had never taken his breath away, and the carved wood had never made him wonder of the craftsmen who had spent a decade putting it together with chisel, flutters, gougers, parting, and veining tools. Albert was, as he realized in that moment, a changed man. He looked down the long expanse of the dining table and its gauntlet of chairs. The room had its own horizon and the table seemed to taper in the distance.

Albert sighed as doors were thrown open at the far end of the Dining Room.

An attendant entered and announced: "Your Majesty. Your Royal Highness. Presenting Governor Moody and the Joneses." In walked the governor, Annie, and Linda. The attendant bowed his upper body and head, and then closed the door as he retreated. Both ladies were dressed in summer dresses, visions of flower-covered beauty.

Linda and Annie quickened their steps toward Albert. He threw his arms up in a V and brought them down to embrace Annie as she jumped up at him. Governor Moody did a dignified stroll over. His suit was crisp, and his hair trim and groomed. He bowed his head as he approached the King. King Edward offered his hand and Governor Moody shook it.

"Your Majesty, I have spoken with the PM. Despite the fact that Argentine forces now hold the islands, and they walk its land and smell its air, we *will* get the Falklands back." As usual, Moody wasted no time.

"Yes, yes. Of course we will. Your Excellence, Governor Moody, I must thank you; Thank you for delivering my son back to me."

"Of course, Your Majesty," Moody said, but quickly turned his attention to Albert. He smiled broadly.

Here was the boy he had seen so distraught, so tortured, now being hugged by two lovely ladies, and with a beaming smile that stretched his face to new lengths. When Annie and Linda finally released the young Prince, Governor Moody went to him and shook his hand. Then he pulled Albert in and gave him a hug, too.

"I'm proud of you, Albert," Governor Moody said. King Edward seemed to take notice, a mix of surprise and jealousy on his face. Attendants entered with steaming pots of Darjeeling and Earl Grey tea, as well as sandwiches—

cucumber and butter, tomato and cheddar, salmon and country pâté.

"Tea is served," was announced. They all approached the vast table.

"An airplane could take off from this thing," Linda said as she adjusted Annie's chair. The little girl placed her chin on the thick wood.

Before Albert sat, his father took him aside, and, as if embarrassed by the admission, said: "I am proud of you, too." He then embraced Albert, his last remaining son. While the hug was not strong and did not pull Albert in tight, Albert used the moment to rest his head on his father's shoulder, to close his eyes, and feel as though he was finally home. He felt his father gently push him back, as though saying: 'Control yourself.' Albert straightened up, gave the well-practiced terse smile of royalty, and made for the table and the afternoon tea that had been set by the attendants.

Albert squinted to see through the clouds of dust that danced about. They twirled in pillars that climbed skyward. Albert smelled baking bread, and though the sun was blinding, he found he could look right at it. Filled with diamonds, the sky sparkled. Despite the wind, Albert could only hear his own deep breaths as he walked. He climbed over the lip of a hill and looked down upon Jugroom Fort and the Afghani village.

Donnan and the little girl stepped out from the hut beside the burnt-out wreckage of the missile-torn SUV. Donnan was in his flight suit and the girl wore a long, colorful dress, a piece of cloth wrapped about her hair. She carried a teddy bear. Both looked at Albert for a moment. Then, both smiled and waved.

Albert gasped awake and sat up. He breathed heavily and found himself drenched in a cold sweat. The tick of the clock was deafening and rain drops pelted the old window pane. Balmoral was surrounded by a moonless night that made the shadows in Albert's room especially dark. Albert looked to the large chair that occupied the corner of his bedroom. He was certain there was someone seated upon it. Exhausted, he ignored the vision, and laid his head again on the cool, silk pillow cover.

There was a knock at the chamber door. A muffled voice asked Albert if he was okay. It was Linda. She knocked again, and pushed the door open.

EPILOGUE: GRITTED TEETH

"The British won't fight."—General Leopoldo Galtieri

Comodoro Rivadavia Military Air Base was abuzz with activity. Fighters—Fighting Hawks, Mirages, and Pampas—flew south to form combat air patrols over *Las Islas Malvinas*. Transports, too, moved supplies and troops there. Dr. Amsel and President Valeria Moreno awaited the arrival of the jet bearing the body of Vargas and other casualties of the invasion and initial occupation.

Amsel nudged the wheels of his chair to better view the preparations of the honor guard and band. He closed his eyes and thought back on all the men he had witnessed marching proud and clicking heels. As passionate as they had been, their passion did not always win wars. Valeria

271

adjusted her dress and shifted her high-heeled stance. She had wanted to be a veterinarian, to care for the animals she had loved so, but her father had clipped the wings of such thoughts, and pushed her to his world. Amsel felt momentarily sad for his little *leibchen*, however, his narcissistic mind would not allow such compassion to linger for long. There, on the wind-swept tarmac, Amsel decided he would do anything—anything—this time around for victory. He spotted the approach of the Fokker F28 Fellowship utility transport.

The F28's twin engines, mounted either side of its T-tail, whined as the jet nosed up and prepped for landing. The aircraft had *Fuerza Aérea Argentina* painted atop the short row of windows that lined its fuselage. Coffin after coffin filled the F28's cylindrical cabin. Each was flag-draped, and each awaited family to cry over them, and for their nation to welcome them home. Inside one of the plain, wooden boxes rested Major Ezequiel Vargas. The F28 settled onto the runway with a puff of smoke from its wheels.

As he watched the small transport jet roll out, Dr. Amsel swore: Prince Albert, his family, and his country would soon all pay dearly.

His Majesty's Ship *Queen Elizabeth*—the lead in a new class of British aircraft carriers—took shape in the dry dock of Scotstoun shipyard on Glasgow's River Clyde.

Queen Elizabeth was a multi-colored montage of individual superblocks, a Lego kit of individual pieces that comprised compartments, pipes, wires, and purposes, and that would become the United Kingdom's largest warship. Over 70,000 tons when afloat, *Queen Elizabeth* stretched longer than the Houses of Parliament, used more steel than Wembley Stadium, and sported towering islands both fore and aft of her immense flightdeck. Two men—both old friends—strolled along a steel walkway overlooking the docks, quays, and workshops of the shipyard that was building these new goliaths.

Admiral Sir Reginald Nemeth was the Royal Navy's First Sea Lord and Chief of Naval Staff. In uniform, he was, despite his age, in obvious good shape, the product of daily workouts and morning runs. Sir Reginald was also very angry; angry at the bean-counting bureaucrats that left Britain with a gap in carrier power. Despite this gap, Admiral Nemeth swore that Argentina would regret her decision; a decision made with more heart than mind. He would lean the full weight of an old first-world power against an enthusiastic, if misguided, second-world one. The other man, the one strolling beside Nemeth, sashayed with his hands clasped behind a crooked back. He, too, embodied anger.

Although a shadow of his former warrior-self, he, too, would fight. He was many gin bottles away from the youth he had been, and—despite the condition of the flesh downstairs—the membrane upstairs was as formidable as it had ever been. Having traded his Royal Navy uniform for a herringbone Armani suit and big paychecks, he was director of British Aerospace's Systems Surface Fleet Solutions, the division of the company that built aircraft, munitions, and defense systems; a company that was one of the principal providers of hulls for the Royal Navy. Today, however, his suit hung in a locker, and instead, he had clothed himself in blue coveralls. Despite the downgrade of his physicality, this man stood as strong a patriot as ever, perhaps even more so. He focused on one goal: the recapture of the Falkland Islands. Both men wore white hard hats, more symbols of safety than a desire to be safe. After all, times were desperate and thus required desperate measures.

Despite superficial differences, both men called themselves mates. They had known each other since the Second World War, when both were young engineers working on 'Q-ships,' heavily armed merchant vessels that, with weapons concealed, would lure German submarines into making surface attacks. These wolves-in-sheep's-clothing then opened fire. Having faced impossible odds before, these men took stock of their current position.

A former adversary had recaptured a far land that had been fought over before, a land that had taken blood and treasure to keep in the fold. However, they were both certain of one thing: this land was worth both these things again—the fight and the treasure—and the loyal citizens that tilled its soil and fished its seas deserved even more so. The two men paused on the high steel of a walkway. They surveyed Scotstoun shipyard. Beneath their perch was the 229-foot cargo ship *Moon Breeze*.

The dry-docked ship was a beehive of activity. Her black freeboard and white superstructure were being painted haze grey, her white waterline and red bottom: black. Gantries traversed the ship's beam, slinging plates of steel to be welded to a trussed frame that stood proud of her decks. Branched black towers were being mounted atop her bridge. They held domed and flat arrays, each with tendrils of wires waiting to be connected. While this occurred, old familiar allies were mustering too, and their support was in transit.

USNS *Fred W. Stockham* plied the waves of an Atlantic squall. She dove into troughs and climbed the wave faces to the crests, crashed back down and plunged into the seas, a wash of milk-white foam rushing off her bow.

An American container & roll-on/roll-off support vessel, *Stockham* made way as fast as the sea-state permitted, pushing on toward the sunrise. Black like the deep ocean water, and covered with cranes and hoists, her 900-foot length rode up and over the latest pile of water. She slammed back down. *Stockham*'s hull creaked as her bow plowed in and parted the water. Her steel ribs vibrated under the torment.

Activity in the ship's hold hummed as the hull's steel frame quivered like a tuning fork. Within the cavernous space were row upon row of shrink-wrapped aircraft. Toward the ship's stern, sailors braced themselves against the roll of the ship's hull. They peeled back the cover from one of many airplanes that were aboard.

With canted tails that jutted from either side of a single engine's gaping maw, the sleek jet sported a golden canopy above forward-leaning engine inlets, diamond-shaped wings, and a sharp faceted beak. Any opening in the fuselage—the vent for its lift fan, the doors for its landing gear, or the windows for its myriad sensors—was accentuated by saw-toothed, radar deceiving lines. This F-35 Lightning II 'Bravo,' a short take-off and vertical landing version of the new fifth-generation multirole fighter, had been built for the United States Marine Corps. However, at this time, the airplane was needed elsewhere, needed by an age-old friend, and had gladly been shifted from inventory.

Within *Stockham*'s hold, an American sailor sprayed olive-drab paint over the starred and winged roundel already there, over unit numbers on the aircraft's empennages, and the word: 'MARINES' that adorned its tail. When the paint had dried, the sailors applied new stencils to the Lightning II's radar-absorbent material, and began to spray colors. When peeled back, the first stencil left behind a red, white, and blue bulls-eye that, through history, has graced Avros, Bristols, Sopwiths, Hawkers and Supermarines, and British Aerospace, and Eurofighter aircraft. With a whiff of polyester urethane Jet Glo Express, this proud bulls-eye now shined on a Lockheed Martin creation, and it would shield an island. Proud of his work, the sailor waved away help from another, and chose to apply another stencil by himself. He carefully taped it into position on the aircraft's tail and sprayed the body of the F-35B. The sailor removed the paper outline. He revealed the name of the new owner of this Lightning II:

'ROYAL NAVY.'

Printed in Great Britain
by Amazon